Columbus Park

N E EVANS

Chronicles Series - Columbus Park

Published by Valeant Press 2018

ISBN: 978-0-9571009-1-6
eBook:
978-0-9571009-2-3 Apple
978-0-9571009-3-0 Kindle

Valeant Press is an imprint of Dolman Scott Ltd
www.dolmanscott.co.uk

Contents

Foreword

Jobe sat at the entrance of the cave, outside, the forest and mountains stretched miles in to the distance. A sad worrying look troubled him, Heti, his only relative in these parts seemed sad, her eyes welled up as the realisation of loneliness gripped her emotions. Scar had to live deep in the mountains, following an altercation with the human race, despite only scrounging for food he unwittingly placed a price on his own head. Every winter, at least she could spend some time with him as the humans retreat to their warm logged houses, with their four wheel drive vehicles on the drive and fridges full of food ready for the winter.

Jobe and his friends Limpy, Jude, Arco, Bonso and Decon enjoy the early spring weather and discover new and exciting places and animals. Herronetty, the guard of the pond and the enthralling tales that drive the colony forward and teach them to survive.

As you read the story to its conclusion, think of the damaged that we the human race are doing to the planet. We care so little of the way we treat the world we all know and love. Soon Arctic Falls will arrive, this has a worrying tale, the whole of the foreboding country is being depleting year on year, the damage caused by a world of throw away culture and our plastic, ends up in this last truly amazing place. Here Whitely, Shiverly and Sleatly all have the massive decision to relocate due to the plastic poisonous outlook for their homeland. Other characters emerge as they search for a new and clean area to settle down, where food is plentiful and humans destruction in minimal.

Other stories are available from the Chronicle series, The first book is Fun in the Snow where Major mouse has a major issues as he wakes from his winter slumber to be greeted with Snow, a concept he was not used too. Floods of Thaw is the second book, where the colony struggle to recover from the thawing snow. Valeant, is a tale of heroism in the face of battle but who comes out on top?

Visit the web site for updates on further publications **www.nutwoodgrove.vpweb.co.uk**

Columbus Park

—— **Chapter 1** ——

The Beginning

Jobe stood nervously at the cave entrance looking out across the park, his mum had already left to go to the nearby river. Each morning she went to catch the trout for their early morning feed. The last wafts of winter blew across the wilderness, snow covered the mountain tops: In the near distance Limpy the hare, Arco the racoon, Jude the Meerkat and Bonso the Beaver all played beneath the old fir tree. Jobe ventured out, looking sideways, the grass beneath his paws was strange, before the winter arrived the sunburnt grass has a very different feel to it. Once away from the cave he bounded to where his friends were playing.

"Well hello Jobe," said Limpy, "have you come to play now your sleepy winter is over?"

"Yes, but you have been asleep too, haven't you?"

"No, far too much fun, to sleep through the winter, besides it's only bears that hibernate, we play in the snow, it is so much fun."

"What is this snow you talk about?"

There was an excited snigger from the group, as Limpy ran round the tree,

"Jobe don't know, Jobe don't know about the snow, Jobe don't know about the snow."

Just then Heti, momma bear, rumbled back from the river,

"Jobe what have I told you about leaving the cave without me, you know that danger lies in the wilderness."

"Sorry mum, I wanted to play with my friends."

"Friends, when they make fun of you like that!"

"It is ok mum, I know about the snow; it is white rain, normally cold like when we went in to the cave months ago."

"Ok, come and have your fish, then you can, if you want to, come back to play."

"Yes you go and have your fish Jobe, do as your momma says." Limpy said.

There was a disapproving nod from the rest of the animals as both Heti and Jobe went back to the cave.

"What? I was only having a laugh, I quite like the little fella." Limpy said.

"He maybe little at the moment, look at his mum, that is how big he will be." Arco replied.

Both walked away up to the mountain cave, Jobe spared a backward glance at his friends and followed his mum back home. From the cave Jobe looked out to his friends, he saw them playing in the sunshine, once he had eaten his fish he was eager to return to his friend,

"Mum can I go and play now, I will be careful?"

"Ok, but don't go far, stay by the tree, so I can see you?"

"But mum, I want to play with my friends."

"I know but don't go far you're still young."

With that Jobe bounded down the hillside, rather excited, and tripped over a branch, he rolled and rolled and rolled, coming to a stop as he reached the tree. All his friends laughed and laughed, he sat up and shook his head, slightly dazed, and promptly laughed off the incident.

"Jobe is silly, Jobe is silly, he can't walk, he can't walk," Limpy sang.

Although a little dazed, Jobe ran after Limpy, they ran, in a playful kind of way, through the woods, after a while they both stopped, rather out of breath

"Where are we Limpy? This is a place I have not seen before." Jobe asked worryingly.

Limpy looked round, to his surprise he had no idea where they were,

"I think we go this way," Limpy replied.

Not overly sure where they were, Limpy hopped through the tree line and Jobe followed, he was sure Limpy knew where they were going and followed without taking notice of where they were going.

The forest opened out to a large clearing, Jobe stood on the edge fearing the open space that awaited both of them,

"Come on Jobe you want to get home don't you?"

"My mum always said in the forests you're safe but do not venture into open spaces, the humans will shoot you."

"You're such a baby, in the open you can see everyone and everything, do you want to get back to mumsy?"

"We have to find our way back, follow me and we will get back."

With that Jobe decided to follow, but he was nervous, very nervous, Limpy, hopped through the long grass not watching where he was going, he tripped over something, and then stopped.

"Wait, don't move, you're not safe."

"Quit trying to scare me will you, you said we were safe."

"That I did, but there are traps all around they are crocodile jaws, they maime and then the humans come and take you away, slaughter you and eat you. There, look, we have to be very careful, follow me but do it slowly."

A rustling in the long grass halted there progress, a whimpering drew Limpy towards the rustling.

There lay a fox, writhing in pain, now Limpy was scared of the fox, they have to run away from them, or they will be eaten up. Limpy saw the fox and was about to run, when the whimper called out to him,

"Please help me, I will die if you leave me, the humans will kill me, please I promise not to hurt you."

Jobe walked over to the fox, the fear was in his eyes, bears will eat foxes, he sniffed the fox, then tried to easy the crocodile jaws just enough for the fox to remove his leg.

Once released the fox limped towards Limpy, Jobe trod on his tail and breathed heavy in his face,

"Don't even think about it, turn and hobble away."

"Later rabbit, later,"

"I'm not a rabbit I am a hare and you will never catch me foxy."

The fox turned away and hobbled off into the distance,

"Come, let's get you home Jobe, before you mother worries,"

They both were very careful through the clearing, and the day was getting old, as they returned back Heti was going spare,

"Where have you been? I told you not to go too far, Limpy, I knew you were trouble, go home!"

They returned to the cave as the sun was setting, it had been an adventure and well, it was time for Jobe to start and grow up a bit, be less reliant on his mum.

"Mum, can I go fishing with you tomorrow, see how you get breakfast?"

"If you want too, let's see how you feel in the morning."

With that Jobe went to bed looking forward to the morning and an adventure to fish with his mum.

The sun streamed in through the cave entrance, Job was so excited he couldn't wait to go fishing. The sun was over the forest as he followed his mum to the river. As they reached the banks his mother sat him down for a pep talk,

"Jobe, you need to sit and listen to me now, this may be an adventure for you, but I have seen larger bears than you, swept away, it looks calm and tranquil but there are dangerous undercurrents that you have no idea where they are."

"But mum, I want to fish, I want to learn from you, so l will be careful."

"Right, look at the water, it is moving that way, down stream, the fish are swimming that way, and some close to the edge, go and stand still over there, don't make a splash, or you will frighten them away. Watch me, and take notice."

Jobe watched his mum gently enter the water, so slow was her movement hardly a ripple broke the surface of the water. Slowly Heti was in deeper water, her paw stroking the surface, then, very quickly she scooped the water and out flung a fish and she bounded to the bank and beneath her paw the now lifeless fish lay.

"Mum, you told me the fish were in the shallows and you were in the deep stuff."

"As I said your too small to be in the deep water, now, gently put you paw in the water, see that rock, slowly reach round it wiggle your claws, slowly now, slowly."

Jobe quickly moved his paw from the rock, and shouted,

"It bit me mum,"

Heti laughed, and laughed,

"It didn't bite you, you scared it away, that's all, it is new to you but you will get better at it.

Heti re-entered the water as she did before, and after several minutes she scooped another fish out and Jobe bounded onto the fish as it wriggled beneath his paw, once the fish was lifeless he gently entered the shallows of the river, he had listened to his mum and found a large rock, gently he moved round the rock and without getting scared he dug his claws into the fish and pulled the fish out of the water. Now he was happy, the days fishing had reaped the benefits. The time had gone quickly and the rewards of the day were taken back to the cave, breakfast time at last. By the time they had eaten their rewards it was nearly mid morning. Round the old fir tree all his friends were playing. Before he was allowed to go and play his mum had serious words with him, about not going too far from the tree, as he was naughty yesterday, he promised to behave and do as he was told, so he could go and play.

Jobe arrived at the tree rather late in the morning; all his friends had been there for hours,

"Here comes sleepy head, mummy not wake you up early?"

"I was up early today mum and I went fishing and caught our breakfast, so there."

"Fishing, I bet mummy went fishing, you couldn't catch me, so fish no chance."

"I can prove it, I caught me a big fish and that is a fact."

"I don't believe you, you can't catch anything, you are too small, not fast enough," Limpy replied.

"I can prove it, you watch me, I can prove it."

"Jobe's going fishing, Jobe's going fishing."

They all went off to the river, he had totally forgotten what he had been told, and was spoiling for another fall. They arrived at the river and slowly Jobe entered the water. In the shallow area, he found a rock and gently felt round the rock, lucky for him one fish now lay in his paw, he slowly closed his paw and the fish was caught. In his excitement he lifted the fish so everyone could see, but in so doing he lost his footing and fell into the deep water that his mum had warned him about, he disappeared beneath the surface.

"Jobe fell in, Jobe fell in" Limpy shouted, dancing round in laughter.

Everyone but Limpy was quiet, and Limpy, looked over to the river.

"Where is he? Where has he gone?"

"That is not good, I have heard about the deep beast, they can swallow anything up, leave no trace, maybe, and they have gobbled him up."

"Don't be silly, he is far too big, we had better go and see."

All of them followed Limpy, to the edge of the river, they were close, and could not see him, now they were all worried, imagine what Heti is going to say never mind do, they were all in a panic.

Suddenly, shouting and splashing diverted their eyes down stream, it was Jobe, he was struggling to maintain buoyancy they all ran to assist Jobe but he was out of reach and out of his depth, every now and again he disappeared beneath the surface which stopped them all in their tracks, then up he popped further downstream. The river turned a corner which slowed Jobe down just enough for Bonso to poke a long broken branch for Jobe to hold onto, Arco, and Jude assisted Bonso to help pull him to the edge of the water.

"Jobe got wet, Jobe got wet, he can't swim, he can't swim." sang Limpy.

"Limpy will you stop singing and help pull him out, before we lose him and then you can tell his mum."

Limpy grabbed hold and they all pulled him safe from the water, but now they were a long way from the old fir tree.

"Mum will be mad at me if she finds out, we have to keep it quiet, do you get that Limpy, don't say a word."

"As if I would, you won't get me saying anything, I never do."

"If you believe that you're more foolish than I thought, you just can't keep quiet." Bonso replied.

"Yes I can, yes I can, you just see, you just see."

"There you go again silly songs you just can't help yourself can you. Look, it is time to head back, your mum will worry, and you will be in trouble"

They all set off returning the way they came, it was a long walk, they did not realise just how far they were away from the fir tree. It was pretty slow, Jobe was still quite worn out from his trauma of the beast of the deep. It had proved one thing, that mum's do know what they are talking about, she had warned him but, well it was an unexpected swim, it did prove one thing, listen to what you mother tells you.

Once again, Jobe was indeed in trouble, Heti was waiting for them at the river's edge, her face was angry, not just with Jobe but all of them, for hours she had looked for them. Jobe looked round at his friends, "Now remember, say nothing or we will all be in deep water."

"We're in deep water, and we are dry."

"Limpy, will you stop singing." Bonso said.

Heti stood on hind legs, her arms crossed, tapping a very angry paw on the ground.

"Where on earth have you been, you just don't take any notice of anything I say, now off with the lot of you, and you" pointing at Jobe "get back to the cave I will deal with you later."

Without another word Jobe bounded back to the cave and all the others went home.

Heti, strolled up to the cave and Jobe sat quietly by the wall expecting a real shouting match,

"Well what have you got to say to me..?

"Mum, I am really sorry I didn't mean to worry you, time just passed, I will be more careful in future, but I was having fun"

"Look, I know you only want to play, I understand, but I worry, it's my job to worry, you're my baby, but your growing up let us say no more but you do need to be more aware of what your doing, I need to know where you are, now your dad is not here, I have to make sure you're safe."

"Sorry mum I will be careful, and let you know where I am, I am tired now it has been a fun day I will go to bed if that is ok?"

Heti, began to well up with tears, her baby was growing up fast, and soon it will be time for him to fend for himself, in the dangerous world. She stroked his head as he fell fast asleep, and Heti sat at the entrance to the cave watching the sunset, it was an angelic time but the humans will soon be back, and that will be a dangerous time not just for bears but for all the animals in the forest.

Chapter 2

A time to learn

It was quite late in the day when Jobe woke, a bowl full of fish awaited him and he was aching a little, he enjoyed the fish and asked if he could go out. After another few words he was allowed to go and play. Not everyone was out Bonso had a previous commitment so it was a little fun in the woods but nobody really felt like going too far today. The memories of yesterday were still evident to everyone, and for a change Limpy was quiet. He did not feel like singing today. The day was quiet and slow, it was a reality check, things, bad things happen and sometimes we get away with it, others well, nobody wanted to know about the others. These are silent and scary things but at least they all were safe, and a little extra vigilant as the days pass by.

The sun was high in the sky, it was early for the heat to be evident but all the snow on the mountains had gone, the ground, though early in the season, was already dry, since the winter had passed the rains had not come, the ground was quite dry, but clouds on the horizon promised a shower or two overnight. Still feeling worse for wear after his untimely swim, Jobe decided he needed an early night. It had been an experience but swimming was not something he wanted to do in a hurry. He bid farewell to the others as, still young, he needed sleep to build up his strength. Mum had always told him he needs to grow big and strong because when he is alone he needs to be able to look after himself.

Back at the cave he sat by the wall contemplating the fact that one day he will need to look after himself but that was a while away, and whilst he was young he wanted to play as much as he could and learn from his mum.

"Mum, how did you learn to look after yourself, and why is dad not around?"

"Listen, you will learn from me and your friends in due course, As for your dad he had to move on, that is what they do I will keep you safe and in time you will be able to look after yourself just as I do, you will move on in time you will have little choice, but I will always be your mother".

He sat quietly for a while, he could not remember what his dad looked like, it was a struggle to even remember if he had even seen him. Jobe snuggled up in his bracken bed, his head full of thoughts about his dad, everything was quiet. The showers that were promised by the ever increasing cloud cover, never arrived, the warmth of the evening had dispersed them. As the moon lit the entrance of the cave up, Jobe slipped off to dreams of his father, he tossed and turned but the memories of his wayward father were all too distant and the night took his eyes.

The spring sun exploded into the cave as Jobe opened his eyes; his mother was just leaving for the river, Jobe called out to her,

"Mum, wait, I want to come with you again, learn how to master the art of catching fish"

"Really, there is plenty of time to learn, but if you want to, come on then, before all the fish have swam away."

Jobe bounded after his mum who had a head start. As he neared her once again he tripped on a branch and rolled down towards his mother who was unaware of his trip. He rolled and rolled, faster and faster, then bump, he ran into his mother and bowled her over in the process. They both rolled down to the edge of the river where they came to a standstill, much to the delight of Limpy and friends.

"Jobe can't walk, Jobe can't walk, he is silly, he is silly, Jobe can't walk"

Jobe got to his feet and ran after Limpy, but he was far from slow, he was like a rocket, so after a short while Jobe gave up and returned to his mother.

"I don't' know why you bother with that hare, he is trouble you know."

"Mum, he is my friend, he may be trouble but he knows about things and you said I have to learn, he knows about humans and that they kill animals. These are the things I need to understand, is that what happened to dad, did the humans hurt him?"

"Not exactly, it was the other way round, you see we live here and in the summer they hang about and offer food, but they lie and the little humans are horrible, one time some little humans chucked stones at your dad, and it made him angry, he growled so loud everyone heard and he chased the little humans. Don't take this the wrong way but they told lies and men with guns followed him, they shot him but he survived but he can never come back. He lives up there, in the mountains, he has a quiet life now and we all know the story but we also know the truth, one day you may see him, but not right now, when you're big and strong you can then make up your mind."

"Do you ever see him?"

"Yes I do, how else do you think you are here, but that is a story to be told later, when your old enough to understand, till then you need to learn from me and your so called friends, it is good you know a little but, knowledge is often gained over time and then you will be an adult."

Jobe took the words of his mother and listened to her instruction, he was not in the mood for another swim, they caught a few fish though the river was empty today, food was scarce at times but other vegetation filled the gap, Heti was a good forager, she gave lessons to the other bears, when food was short, her mother was a master in the art and Heti was eager to learn when she was small.

Limpy and friends had returned. They kept their distance for a while but they all knew he was only playing, and well youngsters will have arguments but they are never that serious. The sun was high in the sky, it was the warmest spring for many years, it was also drier than normal, although the winter had been colder the rainfall was very low and the ground was already dry, the green plants were struggling to grow and the trees had began to lose colour.

"Mum can I go and play for a while please?"

"Yes, but remember not to go to far from the cave, I know that friend of yours like to wonder, look at last week, you could have been hurt."

"I will be careful but I have to learn about things like that, they are wise enough and I want to be wise like they are, so, I will take care."

With that Jobe bounded off to catch up with his friends, it will be yet another day of discovery and he was in no mood to go swimming again.

"Guys, come on let's play."

They all ran into the woods, it was nice to be a cub, the learning part of life can always wait, it is early in his life and time for fun he thought.

Bonso was not with his friends and Jobe was wondering where he was,

"Where is Bonso? I wanted to thank him for the other day."

"Busy busy, busy as bee, building, building, building happily." Limpy sang"

"Building: Building what? He lives in the water what can he possibly be building?"

"The water is going to run out if he don't build, that is what he does, and then the humans take it away, it is an endless job his building.".

"What is he building, and why would he keep doing it, if the humans take it away?"

"Barmy barmy, needs his own army, Bonso, Bonso needs to make it grow."

"Grow, I thought he was building, I still don't know what is he's building or growing."

They all burst out laughing at the comments, he was young and they did make fun of him. Arco sniffed the air, and signalled which way the beaver was and where he would be building.

"It is best you come and see Jobe, it will become more understandable that way, it is a difficult thing to describe." said Arco.

They all followed Arco at times he sniffed the air, they were going down stream the water was quite fast flowing as they neared the build, as they neared the corner, it was evident Bonso had been busy, very busy in fact. Jobe looked across the water and there on the other side of the river was Bonso, in his paws were twig after twig, he had a pile on the bank. Bonso saw his friends on the opposite side and slipped into the current, silent was his entry; Jobe began to run, calling out to Bonso,

"Quick Bonso is drowning, come on, we need to save him."

"Jobe is barmy, Jobe is barmy, he doesn't know, he doesn't know."

Just as he reached the waters edge Bonso appeared from the water, Jobe slid to a halt,

"What are you doing Jobe, you know what happened the other day, and now you're doing the exact same thing, will you never learn."

"But you were under water, I thought you were drowning, you helped me I just wanted you safe."

"Safe I am safer in the water than out, what do you think these are for?"

He wagged is flattened tail and opened his paws,

"These are meant for swimming, unlike yours, I am fast and agile in the water and can swim for ages beneath the water, so no need to worry about me."

"Jobe is thick, just like a stick, Jobe is thick, and he doesn't know he doesn't know."

"Limpy, will you give your silly singing a rest, Jobe has a lot to learn, just like you did, he needs us to teach him, not scare him off, when he is big and strong he will eat you for breakfast." Jude Replied."

Limpy shook his ears and went quiet for a while,

"Do we eat hare then, mum never said anything about that, and maybe I am hungry enough now."

Limpy panicked and hid behind Arco,

"Don't let him eat me please."

"Will you both grow up, nobody is eating anybody, we are friends and friends stick together, we have to look after each other." Jude said.

"Now come let us show you what Bonso is building, we can explain as we have a drink together, make you understand why and how it helps us further up stream."

They all followed Jude onto the dam, Jobe was not sure it would hold his considerable weight, he waited at the edge but was reluctant to get wet again and this time he maybe not as lucky this time,

"Come on it is quite safe, Bonso makes the best dams in this area, they are so well built it takes the human's weeks to dismantle them besides you're not that big yet."

Tentatively Jobe climbed onto the dam, he was very careful where he placed his paws he was still scared that it would give way beneath him, he looked round and was grateful when they all went back onto solid ground.

"So what is this called, it looks like sticks in a line covered in mud." Jobe said.

"Don't be so rude, Bonso is an artist at work, look how long it takes the humans to dismantle it."

"Jobe is rude, Jobe is rude, and he doesn't know he doesn't know." Limpy happened to sing.

With that Jobe ran after him, but Limpy hid behind Arco.

They all wondered round the other bank of the river, it was quite close to the humans but together they were safe. Bonso invited them all for something to eat and drink, it was an adventure for all of them, and, however, the light was quickly diminishing as they all finished their food

"Come on it is getting late and we don't want to be lost in the darkness of the forest," Jude said and they all followed her to the exit, and across the dam, once safely across they thanked Bonso for the food and drink. They all followed in Jude's wake and it was getting dark, Jobe was a little scared, and the rustling trees worried all of them, except for Limpy, who was, as normal, a pain.

"Jobe is scared, he doesn't like it, and Jobe is scared." Limpy danced and pranced about behind Jobe until Jude snapped at him.

"Limpy will you ever grow up, you're scaring all of us, also letting others know where we are, just try and behave will you or I will be sorting you out."

Limpy screwed his face up and shook his head, but it quietened him down, thus realising that in the woods there were dangers, which made him slightly worried. The sun had almost disappeared and a cool mist began to settle over the trees, shrouding them, making them mysterious and darkening the path ahead. Rustling in the background was scary, they all huddled together, but they kept walking, Limpy was in the middle safe from those noises, but soon the welcome of his cave relieved everyone.

"Where have you all been, sometimes you worry me, it is almost dark, do you know how dangerous it can be at night, in the woods? Heti scalded.

"Mum don't be mad we were together, and we lost track of time, we went to see Bonso and looked at his new dam, we are safe and we look after each other." Jobe replied.

"That's as maybe but you have to learn to be more responsible, you will only get into trouble, look at your dad."

"What's dad got to do with it, I haven't seen him for a long while,"

"One day I will tell you all about it but your safe now and that will be the end of it."

"Ok mum, what's for dinner?"

"Honest, all you think about is food."

She ruffled the fur on his head and got his dinner ready, Jobe sat at the entrance to the cave and gazed out over the mist covered landscape, lit brightly by the moon. It was the brightest moon he had ever seen and the pictures were strange as the mist hugged the base of the trees, the words his mother had said to him, played on his mind, what had happened to his dad and why was his mother so cagey about it !

Once dinner was over and the long walk he had endured sent him off to sleep, where the question surrounding his dad played heavy on his mind.

— Chapter 3 —

Legends of the Past

The morning was bright and soon the sun had burnt the mist off, it was another day without rain, the newly sprouting grass was yielding to the lack of water, trees were slightly browning but growing, the real lush grass lay beside the river, which was, thanks to Bonso and his dam. It was still full and as the fish could no longer escape, it was full of life.

Jude called round to see if Jobe wanted to come out to play, he was up for it, she wanted to take him to her new pad, she was busy constructing a network of tunnels, beneath the dryness of the forest floor, obviously he could not fit down the hole but it was fun chasing her from entrance to entrance, trying to guess which entrance was the next one she would appear from. It was a fun day and they both sat down to chat, over a drink of forest juice.

"Was your mum mad with you last night?" Jude asked.

"Not mad, I don't think, more concerned, she said I need to be responsible, then said look at your dad, but I haven't seen him in ages, do you know why dad went away?"

"No, I heard it was something to do with the humans but, folk don't talk about it, they cannot be trusted."

"What the folk round here, well animals here."

"No, the humans, they are the trouble, they are not careful, they destroy things, look with Bonso, every year he builds a new dam, the humans rip it apart, for their own survival. Many years ago now, Wenlock, who used to own the place where Bonso lives now, the humans shot him dead. They blamed it on an accident, but, we all know what really happened. It was a hot dry summer, and the dam Wenlock built was the best anyone had ever seen. The river almost dried up below the dam, they say he was a master builder, and I guess that was true, but humans don't like not having the river. It was almost a stream, they blew the perfect dam up, and as Wenlock ran away from the explosion they shot him dead, and then danced round his lifeless body. That is why, Bonso, has to let some water through his dam, or they will do the same to him. He knows when they are coming, his friends downstream let him know, because then he can hide away from the dam and well just start a new one when they have destroyed it. Sad to think that it is what has to happen, it takes him many months to build his dam, we get extra water for most part of the year and in the Summer; the humans have enough through the Winter. It is a love hate thing, but if we upset the humans then they come after us. As things stand it works but never trust them, even if they offer you food, run away, and don't trust them"

"So if humans come near us then run away, why run?" He asked.

"One day you will understand, your father had to run, humans were to blame for that."

"What happened, mum would not say either, she told me one day she would tell me but, that is all."

"Best do as she says, she has her reasons and best we don't upset her, she still blames herself, but one day, when you're ready she will tell you all about it, till then, do as your mother tells you and be careful."

With that the conversation returned to everyday talk it was nice not to have Limpy making fun, he was ok just very silly at times, he was funny at times and he wouldn't hurt a fly.

"Jude, do you have any more stories to tell me, like Wenlock, he sounded a very nice beaver, shame he died?"

"There are many tales, that go back years but I wouldn't want to bore you, but as your asking. Many years ago, well before I was born, there was a stag, who ruled this forest,"

"What's a stag?" Jobe interrupted.

She shook her head, and tutted.

"It is an adult deer, don't interrupt, anyway this stag was the biggest most scary deer you ever would have met, he pounded this area and every other deer wanted to fight him, but never did any deer beat him. Each year he would fight to protect every female deer, some of his relatives still walk these forests, but they are not as scary. Anyway, each year when the autumn was nearing an end he lost all his antlers, and even today, some humans pick these up and keep them, not sure why, but they do. Anyway, one early winters evening, it only happened once I think, but one antler would not break off, and his head always lay to one side, it was very scary, and everyone use to run and hide. One of the nice humans, don't trust them, but one of the nice humans shot him, he ran for a mile before he fell to the floor, and then the human caught up with him, got this big metal blade, but full of teeth and it eat through the antler, but then, after a few hours he was spotted running through the forest, and without his antler but his head was always set to one side. The following spring he had grown another two antlers but the human had taken away his spirit, and he never won another fight, in fact he left for the mountains, possibly where your dad went, but never did he return."

"I see, so not only do the humans kill animals but sometimes they take their spirit to, send them into the forest, I see why you told me to run if you see a human, they may take my spirit to."

Jude laughed, nodding her head.

"Quite, yes, if you run then you will be fine, but take time to learn, listen to your mother, she is so wise, and she will protect you with all her might and if you listen one day you will be as wise, if not wiser, than you would imagine."

"Really, do you think so?"

"I know so, but take the time to learn, one day you will thank her for all that she has taught you, it may well save your life."

"I love your stories, and you say they are true!"

"The forest has many stories to tell, some are wonderful, others are dark and scary, we have much to learn from the trees, they are old, so old, some many centuries old. Down in Hollies Falls, lies the biggest oldest tree in this whole forest, the boughs are weakening now, the time has worn away its bark, so have the stags, they have rutted the very soul of the tree."

"Rutted, what is rutted?"

There were a few sniggers at the question but Jobe was still young and had much to learn.

"Honest, rutted is when the adult stags want to learn to fight, to dominant in the forest, prove they are the best, you will see one day, if you go to Hollies Fall, there you will see antlers broken and rotting.

All young deer's will visit this place it is part of their life, you will understand one day maybe you can ask your mum, she is wise and you will be wise, if you listen, take the time to understand life."

"Was my dad wise? Is that why he went away?"

"Yes, he was wise, the humans made life hard for your dad, if he had not been wise, you would not have a dad, he decided to go to the mountains to save you and your mum, the humans wanted him gone and he went to save you"

"How is it, you know all this, and mum never told me?"

"To protect you, your young and need to listen to everything you are told, one day you will need to look after yourself, to survive, to make your own way."

Jude decided it was time to sort out some food, to forage for something to eat, the day had passed quickly, and after all the talking her throat was dry.

"Come, let us get some food I could do with a drink as well, what do you like to eat Jobe?"

"I am not fussed, mum makes me eat fish but mushrooms are nice to eat."

"Mushroom soup it is any other preferences?"

There was no other request and off she went, Jobe sat by the bush and waited, it seemed ages but soon the return of Jude brought a few other guests with her. She had a basket full of different types of mushrooms, and some homemade berry juice, which looked lovely.

The day had passed quickly and the afternoon sun was low in the sky, it was time to head back to the cave and after the last episode in the darkness the thoughts of that were very clear in Jobe's mind. It was, had been, a nice day and the stories told, were enjoyable, but Jobe wanted to get back to take in all that he had heard, learn what he could from his mum.

When they arrived back it was a beautiful evening, Heti and Jobe sat watching the sun go down, the stories of the past played on his mind, he wanted to know more about his dad and the reasoning behind his departure into the mountains. He contemplated on asking his mum but realised that last time he asked his questions upset her. His decision was to wait a while, one day he will be told of the reasons but until that day came the questions would remain in his mind.

The following morning was bright and warm, it had been a very dry start and the heather was browning, the river was not as full as previous years, all the animals feared the dryness, the inability to consume vast amounts of water and, the red mist was looming.

Now the red mist was another story, the last time the red mist took hold many animals died in the southern forest, trapped and burnt their charred carcasses filled the air with a stench few remembered but stories were told by those who did survive.

Limpy called round in the early morning, to see if Jobe and Arco wanted to play, it had been a day or so since he was round these parts, it had been nice not to have his silly voice always making fun but he was missed when not about,

"What shall we do it is a nice day and we can stay out all afternoon,"

"Can we go to Hollies Falls?" Jobe asked. After the stories told yesterday, it would be nice to see the story.

"Wouldn't want you to be scared Jobe, it is full of ghosts"

"Ghosts, I may be young Limpy but seriously, ghosts, I think your scared, that is why you make up the stories you tell, make fun of animals, when you get scared."

"Honest you pair are like children! come on, I have been there many times and never seen or heard of the ghosts, it has antlers that's all and the tree is old, it creaks when the wind blows, there are no ghosts."

"Come on it is a fair walk but we have all afternoon, there is a short cut but we have to cross a clearing and if humans are about we may run into trouble so we keep away from the clearing"

As they all went off to Hollies Falls, Jobe was excited, the story told of the old tree, and how the rutted bark and broken antlers. It was going to be great. The path was a little overgrown and some of the bushes seemed to claw at the travellers, it was not an easy track to follow and as the trees thickened it caused a dingy look to the path. Limpy moaned and mumbled, to himself, at one point he ran in front of Jobe just so he was not behind but when the undergrowth eventually opened out he dropped back and danced about, his normal silly jargon was silenced, he did look a bit peaky.

At last they came to the man made amphitheatre where the vast aged tree stretched out to embrace all that came to see. Piles of old and rotting antlers littered the ground, some so old they were almost buried, but what an awesome sight it was, though at this time of the year it is always quiet. When the trees are fully laden and the rutting season begins the noise was overwhelming and it was loud, so loud, but all the stags came to fight, as a gentle breeze brushed the tops of the trees it was clear you could hear the tree creak "Magnificent, what a sight to see, we will have to come and watch them rutt, when it is time."

"Not a good idea Jobe, many animals are trampled on, when they rutt, they just want to fight and if you're in the way you are trampled, and maimed, best keep away that is what I advise, your mum would go spare for she could not protect you."

"Oh, is it that bad?"

"Worse than you could ever imagine, even your dad would not come here in rutting season."

"Well, there you have it, Hollies Falls it is a sacred place for deer's and we have no place in it, this is the last place you would want to be. Come, we can explore it but just be careful."

They all followed Arco down into the amphitheatre, it was quite steep but once there it was awesome, the bark of the tree was scarred, bark peeling off and antlers by the thousand, the wind blew stronger and the boughs of the tree growled, it was scary to a point,

"Watch you don't get eaten, or you'll be beaten," Limpy skipped round the ageing tree,

"Back to normal, are we Limpy, who has rattled your cage?"

"Cage, what cage? Are you seeing things Jobe?"

"Seriously, it is a figure of speech, really you are kids, grow up, this is educating Jobe, all this knowledge will help him in the future and you Limpy would do well to take notice, not take the Mickey,"

"Mickey, who is Mickey?"

Arco shook his head in disbelief, what we have to put up with, he thought, one day he will be sorry being a tease.

"Right, time to head back, it is a long journey and soon it will be dark, we have to get back safe, stay close, don't want to lose anyone, especially if it is dark."

They all clambered up the steep embankment, once at the top they gifted a longing glance at Hollies Fall's, it had been an educating day, to see the ancient tree, to see where the deer's rutt and fight for glory, but eerie when the wind caresses the old ageing boughs of the oldest tree in the forest.

Once Hollies Fall's were out of sight, the forest seemed to close in, the dimming light created interesting shapes and some scary moments, it was a pleasant journey back and soon the cave became visible and Heti waited at its entrance.

"Have we had a good day then?"

"Yes mum it has been interesting, it was nice to see the oldest tree in the forest, it groans with the wind you know."

"I am aware of that; did they explain why it can only be visited this time of the year?"

"Yes mum, they told me, and the reasons why, so don't worry, I have no intention of visiting any time soon."

"Good, at least they are teaching you things they should and now I think it is supper time, then bed, we have a special day planned tomorrow, so get some sleep."

"What special day?"

"You will see, don't want you excited or you will not sleep."

Just the mention of the special day had excited him, but after the long walk from Hollies Fall's, he was tired and as soon as he lay down he fell asleep.

—— Chapter 4 ——

A Surprise in store

Jobe was woken up by a shake,
"Come on son we need to get going, we have a long walk ahead of us and we don't want to be late"
"Late, late for what?"
"You will see, I told you it was a surprise, come on."
Jobe followed closely behind his mum, the sun was barely visible on the horizon, it was very early in the morning. Jobe shivered as they walked through the cool morning mist, he was far too interested in following his mum to notice where he was.
"Mum, where are we going, we are a long way from home and I have not been here before."
"That is why you're with me, you should be keen to see where you are, I hope you don't need to come here, it is possibly the wildest area in the forest, never come here alone, not till you are an adult."
"Then why are you bringing me here today?"
"Be patient son, all will become clear, soon enough."
The forest began to open up, a clearing became visible, Jobe hung back a bit, scared of what lay in wait in the clearing. Heti, turned, she saw Jobe begin to stop.
"Jobe, what is wrong, come on we will be late,"
He was scared only a few days ago the clearing almost claimed a life, he shook his head.
"Mum, the clearing is full of dangers, crocodiles lie in wait, they bite."
Heti walked up to Jobe,
"Who told you that? There are no crocodile here,"
Jobe knew he would be in trouble if he told his mum of the clearing when Limpy got them lost.
"Stories mum, they say in the clearing the steel jaws wait for the innocent, claiming lives of rabbits and fox,"
"Oh, you know of the other clearing, you are right, but up here, we are away from the humans, they dare not enter this place, don't worry, trust me."
Jobe was still scared, he was but a step behind his mum, and when the bushes rustled, he clung to his mum.
"I am scared mum, what was that? Over there in the bushes, the humans are after us."
"Scar, is that you?"

From the bushed strolled a familiar face, but from a long time ago, as the big brown bear got closer Jobe realised who it was.

"Dad, is that you dad?"

"There are no flies on you son, look how big you have grown, you have your mothers eyes."

"No I don't, how will she see without eyes,"

There was a rapture of laughter from Scar, and Heti smiled and hung her head.

"Heti, so nice to see you, it has been a while how are you? Every morning I pray we can be together, as a family, but we have to make the best of the times we are together. I miss you, a lot, we have young Jobe and he is growing fast. I hope he is not causing you to worry."

"He has his moments, but he is learning, and fast, he can fish now and he has friends. I can teach him basic survival but he still needs to learn from you, you have a special way with him,"

"I will get to spend time with him, but he is young and you are the best mum in the world. I will arrange some time, I don't want him to end up like me, you need to explain why I have been chased here to this remote place, not today but soon."

"I will, when the time is right, before he suffers the horror that you suffered, he can then live a better life, a safer life, and not be faced with human revulsion."

"So Jobe, what do you want to do, we can talk or you can learn new skills, life skills, those that otherwise you may miss out on."

"I want to learn dad, from you, understand why you live here, so far away, be able to hunt and survive like you."

"All in good time my boy, all in good time. We will start with concealment, the art of invisibility, so you can be safe away from the humans. Look I will close my eyes and you hide, I will try to find you, go on, and scoot."

Jobe excitedly ran off to hide; he thought he would hide in the grass that was a good place to hide. This gave both Scar and Heti a few precious moments together before they went to find him.

Jobe hid quietly for what seemed ages before he heard the footsteps of his mum and dad, he rustled the bracken as they got close, but they chose to ignore the noise pretending to pass him by, both doubled back to surprise Jobe.

"Boo,"

Jobe spun round to see the laughing faces of his parents,

"Well done Jobe we missed you the first time, you just need to remain absolutely still, or people, humans will hear you. Good effort, you will soon learn, one day you may be able to stop over, you and your mum, we could bond."

"Bond, is that like glue?"

"Similar, but we would begin to know each other, think like each other, be one together."

"When dad, when."

"Soon enough, your mum and I will sort it out for you. Now, close your eyes, count to ten then come and find me and mum,"

Jobe began to count, Scar and Heti went off into the woods and up the hill, he was in full view but once again they could spend precious time together, it was magical, but they kept an eye out for Jobe.

They both returned and hid just a little, but rustled the bushes as Jobe neared, he jumped about in excitement that he had found them.

"Well done Jobe, you found us."

"Just one point dad, remember to lie absolutely still, people, humans will hear you rustle the bushes."

They all laughed out loud, it was a great day, but time was getting on,

"Jobe, come we need to make tracks, it is getting late,"

"But mum, I don't want to go yet, I am having fun, can we not stay?"

"Soon son, very soon, when you're bigger, and stronger, we will stay longer."

Jobe sighed and turned to his dad, they all hugged, it was emotional but time waits for no one it was time to get back.

They both set off back home, they turned briefly and waved then it was a long walk back, it was also getting dark. Jobe was quiet all the way home, he followed his mum closely as the night descended on the forest, it was lucky the moon was bright, it lit their way and soon the old fir tree came into sight, they were home.

Once in the cave they had some food,

"You're quiet son, are you ok?"

"Yes mum just tired I guess, it was nice to see dad, why could we not stay?"

"You will understand soon enough, there are many things you need to learn first, but one day soon, we will stay a while with your dad, it is complicated at the moment, be patient."

With that Jobe curled up and went to sleep, it gave Heti, time to reflect on the day and those special moments with Scar, the future was uncertain but looking brighter. She sat at the entrance to the cave and stared out across the forest, the sound of the night echoed in the tranquil evening air, it had been a good day, she just wondered when, if ever, they would be together as a family, but that was the last thought of the night as she lay down and fell fast asleep.

Jobe woke early and went in to see his mum, she was fast asleep, he decided to be brave and try and catch his mother a few fish for breakfast. He had been told not to go fishing on his own but following yesterday's trip he wanted to do something nice for his mum. It was still quite dark, time in the forest was only measured by the rising and setting of the sun, which was all well and good but when the clouds obscured the sun time was irrelevant. He did remember most of what he had been taught, he was not wanting a further swim, besides he was alone and his friends were not there to drag him from the monster of the deep.

Jobe picked a protruding rock to position himself safely on the edge, it was cool and the water was quite cold, he gently teased round the overhanging rock, aware the sudden movement would scare off any fish. Gently he worked round, then he felt the fish wriggle, he clasped shut his paw and eased out the fish, his claws had silence the movement and the fish was his. The same routine was followed a further three times, and proud of his efforts he went back to the cave. As he arrived he gently woke his mum.

"Mum, breakfast, he called,"

She sat up unaware of the time and stretched, she rubbed her eyes, before she was fully awake. A proud smile came across her face that was before she realised what Jobe had done.

"Jobe, what have you been doing, I have told you so many times not to go to the river, what if you had fallen in, where would I be, how could I tell your father?"

"Mum don't be mad, I was careful, you taught me to be careful, I just wanted to do something nice for you, I enjoyed yesterday, and, and."

A tear began to develop in his eye, and he sniffled, his mum's expression changed to a smile,

"There, there, don't cry, I know your growing up now, I worry you know I do, you will always be my baby, and I need to accept that, your dad did tell me not to smother you too much. Thank you sweetheart, we will enjoy breakfast together, a breakfast you caught."

They hugged, and eat their breakfast, the sun lit up the cave as it broke through the clouds of the morning, and it was a good start to the day.

Jobe heard his friends as they played round the old fir tree, he looked at his mum, and a nod signalled he could go and play, he ran down the hill and joined them, it was another nice dry day, the snow had gone from the mountains, but the clouds hid the peak from view.

" What shall we do today? The snow has left the mountain, we could go to Fisher's Pool, if you like, it is nice there we can play in the pool and I can show you my hide. "Bonso commented.

"Fisher's pool, Fisher's pool, only plays there, if you're a fool." Limpy sang.

"Trouble with you Limpy you like to make yourself heard, why do you always sing, and put the mockers on anything, you need to grow up." Arco said.

"I quite like the way you sing, makes light of any situation, but you can be a bit full on." Jobe replied

"It's not cool to be a fool; it's not cool to be a fool. We're all off to Fisher's pool, we're all off to break the rule."

They all followed Bonso, it was another adventure for Jobe, he had never been to Fisher's pool, his mind was active as to how many fish would be there, he had never been but was looking forward to adventure with his friends. Remembering the last time he and Limpy got lost, Jobe took to taking an interest in where they were heading, he did not want to be in that position again. The others were quite unaware of where they were going, at every junction. Jobe marked a tree with his claw so he had an idea where they came from. It was a longish journey, the sound of rushing water indicated that they were near to the pool, Jobe had no idea what was in store for him, something that would intrigue him, and surprise him.

As they rounded a blind corner, the sight of a massive waterfall was not what he was expecting, it was a sight that pleased him but also gave rise to unanswered questions.

"Wow, what a sight, I never expected anything like this." Jobe said.

"The forest has secrets that humans have yet to discover, there will come a time when all this will be spoilt by the humans that ravage the planet. Once they find a place like this they will destroy it with their savageness, their litter, their own self importance. Their interference will be so destructive we will have no chance, we will lose our identity, we will fail to exist, that was something your dad found out, he managed to escape but he is almost a prisoner of the mountain, he would love to return, but dare not." Bonso's words echoed

"Was that the reason for him running to the mountains, mum nor dad wanted to let me know the full reason, they just said it is complicated." Jobe said.

"Look, enough talk about the past, we know the reasons, we understand the reasons, and you will know one day, you are still young but as you get older you will see the hatred the humans bring, we need to enjoy things as they are and then we deal with any issue, later. We are here to enjoy and play so let's play." Bonso replied.

They all began to play, it was a fun afternoon, there was still a burning question which Jobe tried to answer but this was all new to him, it was a struggle to ask the question but it did need to be asked.

"Arco, you know all that water, where does it come from? will the water ever run out? It is a lot of water."

Arco sniggered, but Limpy heard what Jobe asked and couldn't help himself.

"Jobe wants to know, where the water goes, Jobe is a Wally, going off his trolley."

Jobe turned to Limpy and ran after him, he wanted to teach him a lesson, and Limpy lost his footing by the pool and began to slip into the water. Jobe called out to his friends,

"Limpy falling in, the deep monster will grab him, quick help me."

Nobody moved and fearing the worst, Jobe jumped in the water to save him, all the rest were laughing, he panicked, before realising the water was shallow, it was over the far side where the deep monster lived. Once he realised it was shallow he just splashed about, they all laughed, and all joined in, ensuring they kept to the shallows.

Soon the day was growing old it was time to return home, once the light went it will be difficult to find their way back and nobody wanted to be lost, and Jobe did not want to worry his mum.

They found their way to a point but as they came to a junction, a slight panic set in, as Bonso could not remember which way to turn, Jobe, took it upon himself to walk round the trees to both sides, he remembered that he had clawed some trees pointed out his mark, they were a bit unsure but Jobe had remembered so they followed him. Soon they came to the old fir tree, and safety before the night clouds descended and another adventure was at an end.

Another day had elapsed it was quite an adventure and the more adventures they shared the more Jobe learnt, it was good that in his father's absence he got to learn some of the skills that would benefit him later in life.

One thing that did bother him was the humans, so many stories he had heard were worrying, they were reasons why his dad was up in the mountains, but as yet nobody would tell him the reasons. Jobe curled up as the moonlight painted a strange stillness to the forest, wolves howled and the owls hooted, it was a strange night, as normally the night was quiet, but Jobe closed his eyes and drifted off.

Chapter 5
Quiet Reflection

The morning sun illuminated the cave, he rose and stretched, breakfast was on the table and his mum had not said anything about yesterday, which was strange, but Heti was quiet herself, she was not, had not been the same since she and Scar had spent time together.

"Mum, are you Ok? You are sad for a few days, why are you sad."

"Oh Jobe, don't worry, it is sometimes hard when you miss someone, and I miss your dad, he has to be in the mountains, away from the humans who chased him there many years ago. I get sad but we will be fine and one day he may come back, just not at the moment. You are the most important thing to me at the moment, but there will come a time when you are out there in the forest, on your own, you will live your life and who knows what may happen. Anyway what did you do the other day? You were out all day."

"We all went to Fisher's pool, I had to lead them back, Bonso forgot the way, but I had marked the trail so when he got lost I found the way back, it was a nice place."

"I remember it well, your dad and I spent many hours there, that was many years ago, but I still remember it like yesterday."

"It was yesterday mum."

"No silly, I mean it felt like yesterday, to, me."

"I did not see you there, which way did you go?"

Heti laughed out loud, it was nice to see his mum smile, chase the sadness away, for a short while anyway.

Jobe saw his friends by the fir tree, and went to play, a slight backward glance to his mum bore a smile on her face, but once he was out of sight the sadness returned.

Jobe joined his friends by the tree and Limpy was his usual self again, running round and singing daft songs, nobody really took any notice, because they were all used to him. Jude suggested they all go to Staggers Drop, the word stag rung worrying images in Jobe's mind, he remembered Hollies Falls, where the aged fighting of the stags took place.

"Is that anywhere near Hollies Falls, where the stags rut? Jobe asked.

"No, it is the other side of the forest, but there is a tale associated with the place, Years ago, it is rumoured that a stag, running from the human hunters, tried to fly off the top, they said he had antlers of gold, and the humans wanted them as a trophy."

"Yes, let's go there, I want to see this place, did he fly?"

"Jobe wants to go, he's in a rush, and Jobe wants to go, to see the magic bush."

Jude lead the way, Limpy carried on singing and followed closely behind.

Following the problems of yesterday, Jobe marked the trees at every turn, he decided that better to be safe than lost, he did however have to change the marks because they were going a different direction, he did not want to get the wrong trail, if that was needed. It was a long journey and there were a few clearings that needed to be negotiated, the humans were slightly more likely on this trail but, it could not be helped.

The early morning sunshine flickered through the trees where the canopy opened out, a little, it was a nice journey but quite a few twists and turns in the trail. Some of the views were breathtaking and even some sheer drops which gave Limpy a funny turn, it promised to be truly awesome.

"How much further is it Jude we seem to be walking miles and I feel peckish," Jobe asked.

"Not much further and we can call on Thrifty, she lives not far from Staggers Drop, and she will always have something to eat."

"What is she?" Jobe rudely asked.

"She is a very dear friend and I would ask that you are polite to her, she is a squirrel, and a very nice one at that, quick, as lightning she is but one of my oldest friends, be warned Limpy, she won't like you making silly songs up and, just behave, all of you."

A wooded coppice set to the right was where Thrifty lived, she was a legend in these parts, and all the animals did as they were asked, keeping quiet and respectful, it was nice to see the legend and as promised she layed on a feast that covered all tastes.

Due to the time they could not spend too much time with Thrifty because there was still a short distance to go and midday was close to hand. They enjoyed the food and respectfully thanked Thrifty for her hospitality and then continued on their journey. It was not long before they reached the top of Staggers Drop, the view was fantastic and well worth the long trek.

"Right, gather round, this is Staggers Drop, don't be messing about, especially near the top, it is a mighty long drop, and one, nobody would survive, the thick bushes hide sheer drops and branches that will trip unsuspecting animals, then it will be too late to save you. Limpy, don't go running round and expect others to chase you that is what happened only last fall. A rabbit, one of your type was running away from a fox and the bushes swallowed him up, nobody ever found a trace of him, they say at night you can hear him call out to you, it may well drive you mad. Now, listen up, all of you, this is the story of Breezedon, the fastest most notorious stag for many years, they say he lives on in these parts but, partly because he died at this very spot, but nobody ever saw his body, swallowed up by the bushes lost forever in the depths of the forest. Word has it that he had upset the humans in the nearby village, killed the lord of the manor, and his antlers were shining like the gold long forgotten in these very waters. Down there, in the deep damp forest bottom, the river runs, deeper than a full grown grizzly bear, but in the depths the shimmering gold it tempts people to their death, they meet Breezedon, who whisks them to their death."

"Has anyone ever seen this Breezedon? He seems so scary, would not like to meet him at night, you say he lies in wait for humans, not all bad then."

"Make no mistake, he has never been seen but those he takes are heard to scream for hours, not one to be messed with."

For once there was silence, nobody dare speak, but the tale was delivered, and suitably understood.

Jude carried on with the tale,

"It was late in the fall, so many seasons ago, it is hard to recall, the exact season but it was late. the lord of the manor was unsaddled when he took on Breezedon his own foolish pride took him on with nothing but a sword. All his party watched as he fought he got some really great stabbing jabs but then, Breezedon pounced and gored the lord lifting him up and shaking him, till he fell lifeless to the floor, one antler was dripping with blood and they gave chase. Breezedon was swift and they struggled to catch up, but they were just over there, and Breezedon, goaded them to follow him to this very spot, he knew about Staggers Drop, he knew the history and they all followed him, he knew of a path, one that was hidden from view, but they fell to their death and Breezedon, watched as they disappeared, the screams lasted hours, till at last they fell silent.

It was later maybe the next season that he fell foul of this place, it had been a long wet season, the vast amount of water had washed away the edges of the path, that he knew so well. Once again he was goading humans who were still tracking Breezedon, they were family members, they wanted revenge but they had investigated the area, they knew about the path and that it had been washed away. They waited close to that tree, and then gave chase, Breezedon, unaware of the dangers leaped, but the path had gone, he rolled down and down till the river swallowed his broken body and the humans cheered for their revenge. To this day and every season, the humans celebrate the demise of Breezedon but at night they say you can hear him running and the voices, thousands of voices fill the night. They do say if you catch sight of him you will be the next to be devoured."

"Oh, I don't like this place what if Breezedon comes back, we will all perish," Jobe replied.

"Jobe is scared now we must prepare, Jobe is scared, it's not fair."

Limpy ran round in circles before he lost his footing, and began to slide into the bushes, lucky for him Jude, grabbed his ear and pulled him back up, or he would have been the next victim.

"What did I ask you not to do, lucky I saw you, I told you not to run round, this is a dangerous place, and one that claims many lives."

Limpy held his head and mumbled an apology, the day was getting old and the early afternoon sun was warm but time was passing by so quickly, it was soon time to begin the trail back, they all took one last look across the valley, then turned for home. Limpy was so very quiet after his close encounter with the deep, and the tale of Staggers Drop, but he followed closely behind.

The day was drawing to a close as they saw the old fir tree, as they said their farewells, Limpy took Jude to one side and apologise wholeheartedly, he could have been a goner, and he had been saved, this time. Jobe walked up to the cave where his mum waited with dinner ready for him, she was intrigued as to where they had been, they started out so very early.

"Where have you been today, son, you were awake early, I like to know where you're going so if you get lost we have a chance to find you."

"Sorry mum but you were fast asleep, we went to Staggers Drop, and heard all about the lord and Breezedon it was such a scary tale but told so very well. I was careful, they told me it was a dangerous place and to be careful. Limpy, did not listen, he was almost swallowed up by the deep, he was running about and slipped, Jude managed to save him and he was so very quiet on the way back."

"That hare will come a cropper if he refuses to listen and stop running round like a mad hare."

"He is ok mum, I know what he is like I don't take much notice of him when he starts, so I am safe and there is no need to worry."

"I know, you're growing so fast, but you are learning and so long as you are careful you will grow up a fine bear, just like you father."

"Does that mean I will have to run away to the mountains?

"One day we will explain the reason for your dads reluctance to be in these parts, but he will always be your dad, come on let's have something to eat, you have had a long day."

"Mum it has been a good day and as long as you have had a good day, it seems like I leave you alone, I need to look after you."

"You need to be with your friends, they will teach you to survive and I have influenced you in the early years, you need to spread your wings, enjoy being young."

"Mum you do know I can't fly, bears just don't."

 Heti laughed out load, and Jobe laughed with her, the laughter echoed across the forest, as they both sat down to eat. The sun was setting in the distance and soon another day of adventure will begin. Jobe sat at the entrance and was sure he could hear his father's roar. One day, he thought, his own roar would fill the forest with dread but he did not want to be as isolated as it appeared his father was. Jobe rolled into a ball and fell fast asleep.

Jobe woke before the sunrise and sat watching the moon carve strange shadows across the forest, it gave him time to think, to dream of what a normal family would be like. He was immersed in deep thought as the sun broke out across the horizon, he had seen sunsets and sunrises before but this was different, he couldn't understand why though,

"Jobe, why are you not asleep, it is very early and you need to sleep."

"Mum, why is dad not able to come home, I miss him, what did I do that was so bad?"

"Oh Jobe, you did nothing, your father was desperate, and humans were not so forgiving, they did not like some of his antics and wanted to prove a point. They chased him into the forest, shot at him, he was injured and spent many weeks in pain. That is why he is scared, the bullet sliced his flesh and now he is an outlaw, so to speak. What you need to understand is we are wild animals and that the humans challenge, they want to rule the earth but all they do is destroy it, they take what they want and have no thought for us. Forty seasons ago, there was a wild grass fire that devastated the forest, thousands of animals perished the whole landscape was ash and only a few trees survived, but nature compensates for the stupidity of the human race and new hardy plants replaced those that perished. Now a new selfish race of humans exist, the young so easily forget the sins of the past but they have little sense, they are dangerous and you need to understand that they cannot be trusted, not even the little people, they play with flames and soon this forest will once more become ash and who knows, nature may not be able to cope again."

"So, dad was injured by the humans, and now has to spend the time deep in the forest, only being able to visit when the humans are not close by, when the sun is cold, why are humans so nasty?"

"I have no idea but take heed of the warnings, never trust them keep out of their sight even if you're starving, because given the chance they will destroy you and any of your friends. Understand what I tell you and you will be fine."

"I will mum, can we go fishing now?"

"Come on then let's get breakfast."

Jobe bounded down towards the river, his mother just behind him, and as he neared the edge he tripped over a branch and rolled into the water, lucky for him it was shallow and his mum laughed out loud and Jobe rolled in the mud, enjoying every minute.

The fishing was easy because the stream was low, it had been a while since they had rain and even the streams from the mountains were reduced, it was not a good outlook, but from the banks of the river clouds were gathering in the mountains but only in the mountains. After a short time they had sufficient fish and returned to the cave to eat breakfast, it had been quite a morning and once breakfast was over Jobe went to find his friends, Limpy was his usual self calling names and being a pain, Arco was studying an old map he had found in his library, it was a map of the forest some sixty seasons ago, it was all so different and difficult to pinpoint where everything was, Jobe was interested to see what had changed.

They all went to table top, this was where the old forest edges began, a good proportion of the trees had been topped thus giving it the name. It was quite open but because it was in the middle of the dense forest area it was a very safe place and the old tree stumps were ideal to sit round and examine the old map.

Arco lay the map out Limpy placed some stones at the edge to stop it flapping in the slight wind, for a while there was silence, nobody really knew how to read maps, thought Jobe had been shown one and pointed out certain features that assist in reading a map.

Jobe walked round the tree stump several times before he spoke.

"Right, north is that way" he pointed to the headland in front of him, then moved the map so the arrow pointed north.

"How do you know that is north?" Arco asked.

"Well when I was with dad he pointed out that due north will be where the moss grows, as you can see on that stump there moss is growing, so it is north. On the map the arrow marked N is north, so from that it will be easier to find features, even after sixty seasons, look." He pointed out that a thin blue line was the stream he was fishing in first thing, and then followed it up the map and pointed out fisher's pool." Now from those two points we are about here but you can see these dots, they are footpaths, for the humans to read, it tells you what they are here." Limpy scratched his head finding it all a bit too much but Arco was very interested in the map.

"So, we are here and what does that mean, there, it looks like a cloud, does that mean it is where the wind comes from?"

There was a snigger from some of the group, but Arco was not bothered, to him it was a valid point. Jobe, smiled to himself, and looked at some symbols in the bottom left hand side.

"Look, that is the symbol for viewpoint, if I am not mistaken I think that is Staggers Drop, where we went the other day, and look there is Hollies Fall. This is great we can see where we are and so much in this map I have never seen, look, caves, I didn't think we had caves there, we need to go see these, one day and look that is Spring's Breach, right at the top, must be where the streams emerges from the ground. This is great come on let's plan where we can go, so many places to see, and with this map we can find new adventures, we won't get lost so easy as long as we keep certain features in the right places. Arco, where did you get this from? It makes everything, that more interesting, we can plan our days, see new areas, and not get lost so easily."

"It was by chance I did not know we had the map, I was looking for a book and this fell out of the cover of one of the books, I thought it was a treasure map, at first but I don't know how to read maps but it could be a treasure map why else would it be hidden? Maybe we can study it and see if there is anything in that."

"Maybe we can, were there any other papers with it? Like clues, or other descriptive items?"

"Well there was this, it does not make any sense to me but it could be some information."

Arco pulled out the paper that had been scrunched up in his pocket and spread it out on top on the map but it was not something that anybody could understand.

Jobe folded it carefully away in his pocket and they all studied the map, pointing out different features and as a group they all began to understand the way the map assisted and they took turns in finding places that were still visible sixty seasons later. Limpy also took a turn to find out where he lived he was also able to find his home and was happy at that, he ran round the table singing "I can read a map, so I'm not in a flap, I can find my home even when alone."

All of them laughed at Limpy he was a character and that is why they all loved him it was such a refreshing change that as friends they could do anything.

The sun was high in the sky which meant it being about midday they wanted a place Close by to explore somewhere that still remains after sixty seasons but it was difficult to pinpoint one. Jobe traced a line from where they were to identify a small pond that they didn't realise was there, it was not too far away and if they did not know it was there, maybe it still remains.

Jobe led the way through the thicket it was quite overgrown but the track was still slightly visible, so it was easy to locate and in no time at all they were near to where the pond should be. They all looked round but the pond did not appear to be present. Limpy began to sing once again, and run around in ever increasing circles. Jobe watched and listened. "Jobe don't know, where we're supposed to go, we are lost, we are lost." Just then Limpy let out a screech and disappeared from view, next thing they saw was a rather drenched Limpy, shaking smelly green algae from his fur. They had found the pond but it was well and truly overgrown and rather putrid as the smell filled the air.

There was a noise across the water which was alien to them, well not the normal sounds that are associated with the forest it was scary but at the same time intriguing for the group as a whole. Nobody dare shout out they all just listened and the more they listened the stranger the noise became. It was Arco who spoke first, he shouted out across the water, "Identify yourself we are as one and we can win any battle we come across," the others loudly agreed and a rustling in the undergrowth startled a few of them but the stood firm as a group.

Out from the undergrowth a tall grey figure walked out, long stick like legs took big positive steps, a long sharp beak on a little head, it was a strange creature but not scary.

"You referring to me are you, why would I want to battle with the likes of you, I would just fly off." She spread her wings and they were sizable wings alright. "Do you think that even as a group you could stop me, Herronetty I am the queen of this pond and you are trespassing. I have been here more seasons than some of you would remember. It is not very often I get visitors here this is almost forgotten by most."

"That would because they can't find it, you have let it go slightly, look Limpy didn't see the ponds edge, and well now he smells"

"Are, I wondered what the smell was, over there a waterfall exists maybe he can wash the smell away, there it is clean. Can I ask why you are here? It has been many seasons since I had visitors so forgive my brash approach, I never bother to clear away the overgrown weeds, because those humans will come sniffing round and I don't want that."

"I totally agree" Jobe said, "We don't like the humans either; they chased my dad into the mountains, now I don't see him very often,"

"Scar, is that your dad? We keep in contact, I sometimes fly round to indicate any human activity, and then he can go see you and your mum. I like Scar he is wicked, in a nice way, but yes we keep in contact."

"How do you know when he wants your assistance? He is miles away;"

"Not that far, as the crow flies."

"Your not a crow, where are they?"

"No silly, as the crow flies, means in a straight line, not sure who called it crow, anyway, the whisper of the colony always gets back to me, you see many birds and animals, communicate across the unified area and we know of most things that are happening. Anyway being as your here, I the Queen can entertain you, make you all feel welcome. "

"Great, are you going to sing and dance for us?" Limpy replied.

"Most certainly not: I don't sing for the likes of you, I mean you can join me for food and drink?"

They followed Herronetty through the overgrown reeds that sheltered her from unwanted guests, it was strange that the reeds were so high and we all thought we will never find our way back. After a short while the reeds diminishing opened out to a tranquil pond where by its side lay the house of Herronetty. concealed beneath an overhanging rock, it was almost invisible, but nice, and the gentle sound of a waterfall echoed. ,

There was a gasp of surprise at the sheer beauty of the place, it was like a palace hidden from view, a secret garden of iridescent foliage.

"This is gorgeous and so very peaceful, no wonder you want to keep this away from the humankind, they would just destroy it." Jobe said.

"Exactly, that is why this place is secret, and if it were not for the map you found, all the others I destroyed, the less people know the less chance this will be discovered, oh and while I think, you lot better not tell anyone, ever." Herronetty said with a very serious face on her.

"That you can rely on, we like secret places, interesting places, places that the humans have no knowledge of, this map will remain in our hands because we have a vision, we know how lucrative this map is but we will guard it for all animal kind." Jobe had made the promise.

The afternoon sun indicated it was time to make their way back home, Arco called them all together, it had been a fabulous day but time had passed by so very swiftly, Herronetty lead them through the reeds to the exit and pointed them in the right direction.

"Remember, this place is sacred and that map needs to be kept safe, or one day, it will disappear from your hands if word gets out" With that Herronetty was gone and once more the pathway was gone.

They all followed through the woods and pathways that directed them home it had been a day of discovery, but it was a day to remember. Soon the old fir tree came into view, once again the day had been exciting, a day that all would remember for a long time.

Jobe meandered back to the cave, the map secretly hidden, even from his mum, though she already knew, many years had she lived in the forest and much knowledge had she retained.

The morning broke and Heti sat at the entrance to the cage just looking out over the forest, she was edgy, her body language was not the normal calm resounding mum, Jobe was familiar with,

"Why are you sad mummy?" Jobe enquired.

"I am not sad, I am just a little under the weather that's all, did you have a good time yesterday?"

"Yes it was nice, so many places to see and strange animals but you already know them mum, you have lived here many years, but they are still strange. Why did dad have to go away, up into the mountains? Herronetty knew him, and keeps in contact, but we don't see him that often"

"That is because, we live nearer than Herronetty, to the humans, they are still looking for him, and unfortunately that will never change. What you need to understand is that he loves you, us, but the humans have a annual hunting day, and today, well it is that day. Your dad, has gone deep into the mountains, he has no choice, each year they get closer to finding him I fear they are closing in on him, they have new technology that makes it harder to escape capture, but your dad is the bravest and most knowledgeable of all of us. I will be better tomorrow when this day has passed, we will be better. Can you stay close today, the humans may try to chase you if they can't find your dad, and I would like you to stay here with me."

"Why would they want me? I have not done anything wrong,"

"It's not you it is the humans, if they can't find your dad then any bear will please their wanton lust for blood. The humans are destructive race of animal; they have an urge to devastate the world for their own gain and anything along the way. We all live in fear of the havoc they reap, take Breezedon, Wenlock, the list is endless, they annually destroy the beavers work, just because they can, we keep away from them. Promise me, that you will, always keep clear of the humans they only create misery.

"I promise mum, I have seen them with their bright lights, their smoking poles, poles that kill and maim, you have taught me well, as dad has, so don't worry."

Loud bangs echoed in the distance, Heti flinched as she did all morning, rally after rally echoed across the forest, she had a worried look on her face, it was getting all too much for her and Jobe hugged her and they sat quietly, after a while the gunfire ceased, Heti had a sad face and she was troubled.

"Don't worry mum, dad will be ok I know he is ok, he knows the best places to hide, and I am sure that if he was not then we will be informed."

"Your such a treasure and you will make a brave bear when your older, one to rival your dad."

She stroked his head and although she was hiding the fact she was hurting, Jobe, remained with his mum for the rest of the day and night. Neither slept well, Heti kept going to the entrance of the cave to look outside and watched the shooting stars fleet across the sky, and each one was followed by a wish, the moon was large and bright in the distance the night calls of owls echoed, it was surreal, but calming as the sounds bounced across the forest.

—— **Chapter 6** ——
A Learning curve

Jobe joined his friends who were already playing by the old fir tree. He spent a worrying glance back to his mum, her sadness following a few days of worry after the annual hunting day still seemed to remain.

"What shall we do today, does anyone remember the Old Muggleton Farm?" Jobe enquired "I was looking at the map and although it shows it there, and mum has said that we have to avoid any Human contact, has anyone been there?"

"It was rumoured that the old human farmer who was one of the good humans, he used to look after injured animals, he was a gentle farmer who always looked after his animals, and any that needed help. They said that he was chased there following a feud between him and the village and because they tormented him as he has a scar across his face he couldn't live with them anymore. For a while he was the subject of horrible backlash for his own kind and even after thirty seasons he could never return." Jude said

"Have you ever been there, or know of anyone from there?" Jobe asked.

"Well, far be it for me to tell tales, from what I can recall, my second cousin Waterford, he was a beaver like me and there is another small stream over that way. He used to build special dams to divert the water into the path of a big wheel that turned and ground plants and the like for the old farmer. He would keep him safe and then they look after each other. It was years ago Waterford died some seven seasons since and they say the old farmer died at the same time." Bonso bowed his head.

"Can we go see, I know that some humans are nasty well most of them but this farmer seemed to be different he was looking after the countryside and the animals, not all that bad then."

"Ok, but we will need to be very careful, some humans may still be about and they are not all like the farmer and as it was so long since I was there, we may be in danger."

"Bonso, can you take there? as he was your second cousin, we can at least have a look and see, if it looks dangerous we can come back,"

"OK but Limpy needs to button it as his loud songs may be an issue."

"Button it, I have never seen Limpy's buttons where are they kept?" Jobe Asked

They all had a little giggle as they followed Bonzo westerly towards Muggleton Farm, it was a testing route as some unfamiliar obstacle were encountered.

They passed the deserted home of the infamous Draco Marsh, He was in his time a scary otter, he prowled the rivers and caused havoc to many.

"Look here is the home of Draco Marsh" Jude Began, "Since he was a young otter he was attacked by the humans, his sister was killed for her coat and it is said that he went mad and attacked a group of young children, just because they were humans. For weeks they followed his trail, he was cunning and fast, he used to be ok, so I am told, but when he saw his sister killed he was beside himself, went crazy and everyone was scared of him. He was caught some two weeks later and they ripped his fur off just like his sister. You see most humans are nasty but all animals can be nasty too, we have to be so very careful and that is why Muggleton Farm is a bad Idea."

Soon the farm came into view, it was overgrown which was always a good sign as if any humans were about then this would be clear. It was like a ghost house, the slight breeze kissed the old shutters and the wind whistled through the damaged roof.

They quietly walked round the farm, pointing out some of the old cages the farmer used to look after the injured animals. All of them stood amazed at the waterwheel now still, as the water filtered through the rotting timbers.

Bonzo pointed out the special dam his cousin made, which was now in ruins but still intact to a point.

A whimpering in the outhouse startled all of them, it was a strange cry, one most thought was a ghost but as Jobe looked in a familiar face peered back scared at him.

"Don't hurt me or eat me, I am in pain."

"Oh Foxy, nice to see you, best you remain here Limpy is with me and the rest of us,"

Jobe closed in on the fox, and snooted in his face, you stay here till we leave or I will get peckish understand."

The fox coward in the corner and Jobe turned and left the poor animal to his own devices and eased the door closed.

"Was it a ghost Jobe you were very brave," Jude said

No ghost just the wind so come on let's get back the sun will soon be gone for the day and it is a tricky journey back.

Soon the old fir tree was visible again and Jobe wondered back to check how his mother was feeling. After some supper Jobe sat and contemplated the journey and tried to decipher the real human threat. Soon the night took his eyes and he fell fast asleep.

The morning sun filtered through entrance of the cave, Heti seemed so much better, she had already been fishing and on the table, was a spread of fish.

"Are you better today mum, I was worried yesterday, you were not well yesterday, was it dad, he is ok unless something else happened?"

"Oh, Jobe I am fine you do look after me so very well, I heard from your dad, the humans were very close but this time he escaped any injury. He did enjoy our little meeting and we are looking to do it again soon."

" I would like that mum, but the humans are so nasty. We went to see Muggleton Farm, it was ok we checked out everything first and the old farmer helped some animals."

"Are, you should be very aware the humans may have been there, it is true he helped animals. Many years ago, when your dad was shot, he went to Muggleton Farm, for a short while before he had to go into the mountains. He was injured and the farmer helped him get a little better so he would survive the trek to the mountains. If he had not have gone there I dread to think what state he would have been in."

"State, was he leaving the country then?"

Heti laughed out loud such a charming bear and he was growing up fast.

By the old fir tree all his friends were playing and with a simple nod and no pep talk Jobe bounded off towards the tree. He was still young and just wanted to play he was happy his mother felt better and that his father had been in contact, after the last few days of worry he felt better.

"What shall we do today.?" Jobe asked.

"We were close to the humans yesterday I think we should keep away today, there is this place, my sister told me about. Jude Said. "In the middle of the forest lies a bubbling cauldron which bursts through earth and hot water is spread everywhere. It only does it at certain times of the year, this week is that time and we could go and watch it."

"That sounds scary is it dangerous hot water normally bubbles when the red mist fire attacks it, and then all the fish die. I don't want to die neither do you."

"I know about the red mist but this comes from the ground, it is pressurised water from the ground and as long as we keep our distance we will be fine."

They all followed Jude who knew where she was going it was a scary thing they may see but it sounded great.

It was a tiresome walk and after a long walk yesterday it seemed endless Eventually they rounded a bend and a small mound in the distance signalled they were there.

"Jude where is the water then, I cannot see anything but a mound of rock." Jobe remarked

"Give it time, they say it only explodes five times a day and then nothing."

They waited for what seemed like ages and then a rumble beneath their feet startled them all. As they watched the water burst through the ground it went so high in the sky the spray soaked all of them, though it was warm everyone thought it was burning them. As some kind of panic gripped the group, Jude laughed out loud.

"What you laughing at, we are burning?"

"No, you're not it is fine it is only warm water and nothing to worry about at all, but it is a giggle." Jude smiled.

Just then another rumble signalled the second burst of water, as it erupted, they all danced in the spray and laughed, it was a fun day and they all enjoyed it.

Time though had passed by and it was time to return home, it was quite a journey back and it took a while. As they reached the fir tree the sun was setting and the sky was brightly illuminated and this signalled a glorious end to the day, one Jobe really had enjoyed.

—— **Chapter 7** ——
The Red Mist

Heti sat at the entrance staring out across the forest, Jobe stirred and went to sit by his mother's side, and she was troubled.

"Mum what is the matter, dad will be fine, and he will be ok."

"I know he is but there is a far greater threat to everyone, many years ago my mother told me that the forest talks, I know it sounds strange, but she was right, last night deep into the early morning it spoke to me, see, over there, the red mist is approaching, can you smell the mist?"

Jobe sniffed the air, a strange but worrying odour filled his lungs, the red mist pulsated in the distance, Heti was really worried, the red mist takes no prisoners.

"Why do you look so worried mum the red mist is so far away, is it dad, has something happened to him?"

"No, your father is fine I heard back from the forest he is ok, what is worrying, is the red mist is moving toward us we have to make sure we are aware of what dangers are about. The red mist is hot, so hot the trees explode, the water boils killing all the fish the humans will help but they have limitations. Many years ago the red mist took the other side of the hill we moved here to start anew well my parents did, the forest was destroyed and it was the humans who started it, but then they build their steely houses on it, many died, but we are the relatives of that red mist."

"Mum don't worry we are fine, the red mist is many miles away, so don't worry, and dad is fine, besides that is on the other side of the river so it will not affect us."

"I hope your right but if you go and play, don't go to far away, if I lost you my life would be worthless, and your father would not be happy. Now go and play but stay close."

With that Jobe ran to play with his friends by the fir tree, they had seen the red mist but like most youngsters they were not unduly bothered about it. There was some talk of the red mist, but as they study the old map it was forgotten and a whole new area was waiting to be discovered, they walked round a bend in the river, and there was a very inviting cavern, it was barely visible but the entrance was easily found, and it was a nice opening, hidden on all but one side and a small stream meandered through it they all happily played till the night began to creep in, it was time to return home before Heti worried to much.

As they turned the corner panic began to set in, they heard the crackling of exploding trees just over the ridge, and they all began to run. Heti called to them to move away from the mist, but from within the mist flames emerged and the wind fanned them, the outstretched arms of fire reached over the river, it was so very scary. Flames engulfed the fir trees and plumes of red hot mist set nearby trees alight, branches exploded and all of them ran away from the river.

"Stick together don't leave anyone behind the flames will take you, come this way, we need to head away from here, towards the clearing, but still keep together and watch for the crocodiles, we have no choice." Jobe shouted.

"Mum come quickly we cannot stop, we have to cross the clearing it is our only chance."

As they neared the clearing others joined, there was mayhem and everyone was shouting different orders. Jobe let out a loud growl, which silenced the pack, and then he spoke,

"We have to keep calm we need you all to follow the same orders, I am young but we have discovered a safe place, away from the fire, but we need to move as one, take care, for hidden in the ground crocodile steel jaws with bite you and we may not have the time to help you, so be careful."

They inched round the edge of the clearing Jobe picked up a stick trashing out in front of them, steely jaws nibbled the stick but once bitten they present no further threat. The fire reached out taking some of the trees at the edge of the clearing, pushing them quicker but still they needed to be careful. Then one of the larger trees on the edge of the forest exploded, startling the group, Heti turned quickly, and tried to run but tripped on the remnants of winters past. As she hit the floor the exploding tree fell across her, the heat of the flames ripped her fur, her skin blistered but Jobe grabbed her and pulled her free. They escaped across the clearing into the other side but the flames kept following, burning the grass as it crossed the clearing, the steely jaws cracked closed as the wind, a fierce driving wind pushed forth, devastating all in its path.

The clearing slowed its drive but they knew soon that drive will reignite, and the flames will chase once more. It gave them some rest bite and nervously Jobe tended his mother, she was badly burnt but would not give into the fire. They found a small pool where the water gave some rest bite to his mother, but she had a worried look in her eyes.

"Mum, are you ok, you look weary, are you hurting anywhere else, the flame bite you, why would they do that, you didn't do anything to it, but run."

"Jobe, I will be fine, yes the flames took my fur but it will grow back you see, we need to keep moving, soon the fire will return, where are we going"

"There is a safe haven mum just over there we will be safe there the trees are all gone the ground is free of grass, the flames will die trust me, I have read the map. Come let us get there without further injury then I can look after you mum and all of us will be safe."

With that Jobe led them onward and soon the trees opened out, the ground was free from grass and in the centre was an old oak tree, completely alone, a remnant from many years past, a survivor, one most of his friends also knew. Exhausted from the trek they all huddled together beneath the tree, Jobe tended his mum, she did not have the heart to tell him how she really felt, her time was now limited but for today she was fine and Jobe huddled close to his mum to help her sleep. The whole group felt relaxed and safe the fire was burning bright and still the trees exploded, but the wind had turned, the flames began to die out and the smoke choked the moonlight but the group fell fast asleep.

The morning was bright and only a few fires were nearby, there was, in the distance thick black smoke where the wind had turned the flames, still the stench of burnt flesh filled the air. Jobe went to fetch some water to bathe his mother's burns, she flinched as he tendered her wounds but tried hard not to show her pain, and she knew that something else was amiss, she hid the blood coughed up, the tree had taken more than the fur, her energy was limited but she had to remain strong.

"Right, who is going to come with me to find some food, we all need to eat?"

Jobe asked.

"I will come let's go," Arco said.

"Jobe, be careful, the lack of cover makes you both vulnerable, we have to keep safe, the humans may be about." Heti said.

"We will be careful, mum, you rest, and we will be back shortly".

With that they set off in search of food, Heti called one of the small animals over, and asked them to deliver a message to the forest. She whispered the message quietly, to Deacon, and he set off into the forest, but he had little time to deliver the message. Once in the forest Deacon struggled to find a messenger, as most of the trees had been destroyed it took him longer than expected but eventually the message was delivered. With the message despatched he returned to the safety of the old oak tree, but Jobe and Arco had already returned, that raised questions to be answered.

"Deacon, where have you been, I told you to wait here, one simple thing, why would you disappear like that?"

Deacon glanced over to Heti, who signalled not to say where he had been.

"I thought I saw something in the forest, I had to check, make sure we were not compromised, we needed to be safe, the fire still burns and I was only trying to help."

"Fine, thanks, I was out of order, sorry, I know it is not easy, we are but a few here and we have to stick together and that is how we will all survive."

Heti thanked Deacon, but now he carried a heavy burden on his shoulders and it was a difficult situation to be in. They all had some food, it wasn't much but it was something, they were here for a while, as the fire still burnt on both sides it was a worrying time for all of them. Jobe tendered his mother's burns but she already knew it would not help her she was now in pain, but had to remain strong for all of them. As Jobe huddled close to his mother she found it hard not to cry, tears welled in her eyes, she knew her time was short, and that Jobe had no idea of her pain. He looked up at her, to see the tears,

"Mum, are you ok, why are you so sad? Soon the red mist will be gone, and we can return home."

"Son, I am sad yes, I remember the last time we had the red mist, so many animals died back then and I guess this will be the same, all those animals that have been taken by the flames, it will take time to recover. I have seen some of your father in you these last few days, I love you so much, you are a special son, and you will be remembered for all you have done. I am so very proud of you my son, and love you so much."

"When this is over mum I will do everything you ask of me, I have been at times a worry to you, I know and that will change, we can get back to being us."

"I would love that but you have proven yourself to me and you will grow to be a strong bear, one that I can be proud of, your dad too, but there will be tough times ahead, it is so difficult to get back to normal, we will have little food, and we will remember those we have lost to the fire.

Chapter 8

Stories of the Past

Heti continued with the tale,
"I remember the last time we had a fire as bad as this one, the following year we only had the bare necessities, it was a difficult time, it was your fathers undoing to, following the last fire he took to accepting food from the humans, but they are not all to be trusted. Listen to me and listen well, for I don't want you ending up like he did, come it's time to tell you the story of that fateful year, it almost cost him his life."

Jobe snuggled up by his mother, as she began to tell the tale of the humans that stole the honour of Scar.

"It was a day similar to today, the red mist started after a very long summer, not like this, we are barely into the summer but the spring has been so dry. Some humans started it, they were cooking near to the clearing and one of their dogs, knocked the cooking stove over, the hot coals rolled into the shrubbery and ignited instantaneously, they tried to put it out but the grass was so dry they didn't stand a chance, they tried beating it out but it was so dry they just made it worse. They retreated and the heat created a vortex which just stoked the flame, it spread quickly and like you have witnessed, the flames took over. Your dad and I were still young we were told to go to the old pond in the middle of the forest, we had to swim to the island and there we stayed till the fire was out. Many of my mother's friends and your granddad's friends were lost and they were hurting, and it was far worse than here. We had nothing to eat for all the autumn and we needed to eat, your father went to find some food but the only food close by was in the human village. He was careful in the beginning but as time went on he had to be braver and went closer to the human dens. Some small humans started to feed him and he got closer to them, but never trusts them, they lie with straight faces, cause trouble for us, but we had little choice. There was so little food, and we needed to eat, all through the winter months they fed us but the little humans told many lies, and so as we neared the spring we could get more of our own food so he did not need to go into the villages. He sometimes went to the clearing, and rummaged through the bins, it gave us some extra food but those little humans were getting nasty, they often threw the food at him. He retreated for awhile, we managed on the food we had. It was one day, near to the end of the autumn, when some older humans not the little ones, they threw stones at him and some were quite big, and he got very angry, he roared, and then chased them away. After a few weeks, the humans with guns came calling, at first he didn't see them, they presented food but then attacked him, at first he just backed off a bit but then they fired a sharp stick and it cut him. He ran towards them but then the guns came out and as he ran away they shot bullets at him, he managed to escape that time but a few weeks later they returned, in numbers. He ran off but several humans had gone round and he was almost shot, the bullet cut into him and he ran off to hide, they looked for him but he had gone into the mountains and he managed to survive. That is how he got the name Scar. Now they come every year, and to protect us, he stays away, but you can never trust the humans."

Heti looked down to see her son fast asleep, her pain was now severe and she drifted off to sleep, but the pain had began to take her soul, she was so very weak, the burning of her skin had been overtaken by the pain in her chest, but she had to remain strong.

The morning came and the fires in the distance had begun to die, the blackened forest presented a worry, and a return to little or no food for the winter, hopefully the timing of this fire was better placed. Some food will return as we near the end of autumn but it will be a very long and hard winter to go through. Jobe had already gone to look for food when Heti woke, but her condition had become worse, she was hoping that the whispers of the forest had been heard but only time will tell, something that Heti was running out of, and fast.

Jobe bounded back with food and water for the group, he was quite the provider, and she was so very proud of her son, but she knew that unless she improved her time with him will be limited. The time had come to move on, the fire in the distance still burnt across the afternoon sky but they were to head out away from the flames. They all followed Jobe; Heti struggled to keep up but made the effort not to cast any suspicions of the state she was in. Some greenery was evident as they neared the place the fire had turned, but this was an unfamiliar area to the entire group. The fire had taken the direction of the forest and they all just followed Jobe till they neared a safer place to rest, the day was old and the night hung to the clouds that began to close the doors to another day. They found sanctuary where a stream crossed, the fact that there was water and it was needed as a thirst gripped the group, Jobe fetched his mum some water and dressed her wound with leaves, she flinched as the old dressing was removed but the skin so red and sore gave Jobe a worrying feeling, the fire seemed to continue to burn into her flesh.

"Are you ok mum the fire has burnt deep into your skin, is it still burning? We need to get you to someone who can help you, I am not sure how I can make you better, it is so red and you look in a lot of pain, I need to get you to someone."

"Don't fuss so much I will be ok, soon the pain will ease and you will be fine, I promise. Besides we are still in danger, until the fires are all out we need to keep moving, come let us rest for the night here where the grass is green and the fire burns in the distance."

They all set up where they were safest, hidden by the bushes fed by the stream; Jobe went to get some fish and food for the group. Deacon came over to check on Heti, he knew she was not long for this world, but he had made a promise to her to remain positive for Jobe, he would not cope if he knew,

"Heti, are you sure Scar will come, it has been a while, he should be here, with you, for Jobe."

"Deacon, you have to trust me, he will come and then my fight will conclude, but you must look after Jobe, it will be hard for him, but you have seen him he will cope, and you will help him. Scar will come, the forest will remain true, it is written, believe me and he will help Jobe to understand, I have not the strength to do this, his father will."

Deacon nodded as Jobe returned to feed the crew, he was tired, but still he made sure that the crew were fed before he settled down with his mother. Heti was now in pain, real pain, the fire had taken her soul but her fight now was to survive till Scar arrived, it would destroy Jobe alone, she tried to hide the sorrow, the tears. Deacon came with some mushrooms to ease the pain, she agreed while Jobe slept, unaware of his mother deterioration. After a while the pain had eased and she was able to get some sleep for tomorrow she hoped that Scar would arrive, her energy had almost gone and some sleep was better than none.

$$\text{------} \quad \textbf{Chapter 9} \quad \text{------}$$

A waiting game

The morning sun lit the forest with an eerie silence, smoke indicated that the fire was still burning in the east, but they were safe for the moment, hidden from view, but safe in the knowledge that the red mist had begun to diminish. Jobe stirred from a well needed rest, and Heti stroked his head to comfort him, she knew her life was near to an end, but still she had some fight in her if only to survive till Scar arrived. Jobe was busy getting water he had suggested that they move, but Heti was in no state to move, and told him they are safe for the moment and that they all needed to rest for the day, they had been running for too long and all needed to rest. Deacon agreed and Jobe was inclined to agree for today, it was not safe here for more than the day. Although they were staying, Jobe was a little apprehensive, it was close to where the fire had turned and that meant humans were possibly close and he went to check that they were indeed safe, he secured the area and built a covering of broken branches to screen them from any stray humans. Soon the screening process was complete and Jobe was more settled but as he sat beside him mum his thoughts were of her wellbeing.

"Are you ok mum, you would tell me if you were feeling worse?"

"Son you are such a treasure things will work out for you, you are, have shown such commitment to saving these animals you should be proud, your dad will be proud."

"If only he was here, things would be better, he is wise, and he knows this forest, I do not, we are safe for the moment but tomorrow we need to go deeper into the forest, away from all this devastation. The forest is naked and burnt. You're injured mum and I could not stop the fire biting you, now you are in pain and I don't know how to make you better. Dad would know, he needs to come and help you mum, I will go and fetch him, we have to get you better, I need you."

"Jobe your father will come if he can, till then we will be fine, you are such a brave bear, look round at all these animals. They rely on you, you have fed them, protected them, we are safe but as you are well aware we cannot stay after tonight. We need to head into the forest, make a new start. After the last fire we relocated and it took time but we can do it and will do it, a new home is what we need, we will get that home, time will heal the forest, till then we start anew. You will lead them to become self sufficient once more, a new home you will make new friends, some are lost, not all will have survived, but those we left behind will have their own agenda. Bonso lives in the water, he will move upstream, further from the humans but he will be safe, you will see him and the others. Time will heal the forest, it is resilient and a new beginning will start and those we have lost, and will lose, they will remain in our hearts, in your heart. These will look to you for guidance, you are a fine and brave bear, animals will come to you for advice, you may not be fully aware yet but your life will soon begin as an adult of that I guarantee. You will be remembered, for all you have done for these and for me. Sadness may return but I know you are strong enough to cope, you have your father's spirit, and he will soon come and see how you have coped, the forest speaks to him, as I speak to you, he may be in the mountains, but I know he is safe. Soon he will return to the fold but still the humans hunt him, never trust a human, not even the small humans they are the reason your father hides in the mountains, but you are always in his thoughts. Now I must rest I am tired, these last few days have been tiring and I am not as strong as I was, you're my son are my strength for the time being, but I need to rest."

"As long as you are ok I will see what else I can find, we still need to eat."

With that he disappeared into the forest, and Deacon came to see Heti.

"How are you holding up, Heti, you look shattered, is there anything else I can do for you?"

"I am not good, I hope scar can get here in time, I don't want Jobe to face this alone, he needs guidance, if only for a while, he will come to terms with what is about to happen, I hope the forest got through to him."

"He will come; we have to hope that by the end of the day he is here, I will look out for the little fellow if he doesn't make it, of that I will promise."

"Deacon you are a treasure can you get some of those special mushrooms I can't let Jobe see what pain I am now in please."

"Ok, I will go and get some for you."

Heti watched Deacon go and closed her tired eyes, she knew her time was limited but she had to remain strong until Scar could arrive.

It seemed ages before Deacon returned, the only thing that helped manage the pain was the mushrooms, she had to appear in control for Jobe, if he knew, there was nothing he would not do. Deacon returned and promptly prepared the pain relief, he was worried he could see the life within Heti, slowly diminish, and emptiness that only the calling of their ancestors could produce.

"Quick, Heti, take these Jobe is coming back and I can't keep this from him if he asks." Deacon had a worrying look on his face and could not face Jobe.

"Mum, how are you? Are you feeling any better?" Jobe enquired.

"Son, you are a treasure, everything will be ok soon, the pain has eased for the moment, so don't fuss, I will be just fine." Heti gave a smile even though the truth was far from the mind.

Jobe dispersed the food to ensure all were fed, he tried to find Deacon but he was nowhere to be seen, but he guessed he was not that far away, some food was placed to one side for when he returned.

Deacon had ventured into the forest, worried that Scar had not received the call, and sent further messages via the forest. Time was not on Heti's side, he knew soon the darkness would take her and they needed guidance, Jobe was fine, but without his mum, he felt that sorrow would overtake him and then they would all suffer.

A rustling up ahead stopped Deacon in his tracks, he hid in the bushes scared that the humans were close by. As the rustling got closer it was apparent that Scar was close by, Deacon had never spoken to him nor had he ever saw him up close. Nervously Deacon emerged from the brush, and Scar let out a growl, Deacon quivered, and then in a deep and course voice Scar spoke.

"What is the meaning of this call, only my family can use this system, what is this all about?"

"Forgive me Scar, I was asked by Heti to call you, she is in a bad way, the red mist has almost taken her soul and she needs you, we need you. The red mist engulfed a tree and the burning branches took a bite out of her, she is not good, please can you come?"

"Sorry if I startled you, I have to be careful, the humans have yet to forgive me and here it is too close for comfort. How is she coping, and where is my son?"

"Jobe is fine, but he has no idea about his mother, she swore me to silence until you arrive, I fear he will not cope when he finds out, I have supplied her with mushrooms, special mushrooms to help her manage the pain, Jobe has been dressing her wound but still it burns, her injuries are severe."

"Thank you for your support, Deacon, for that I will remember you, come let us walk, then I can think the best way to deal with this. I know it will be hard for young Jobe but I have heard, all the good things he has done, his mother will be proud, as I already am, only time will tell. Everything rests on how I can break the news to him without breaking his heart. You say that the light in her eyes is slowly fading, does she know her life will soon end?"

"I feel she is aware and I have not been able to face Jobe, for fear that the truth will destroy his confidence. He know that Heti is not her best but she tells him she is ok, it will be difficult for the youngster but he has a big heart,"

"That will be his saviour in the weeks and months ahead, I still have to live in the mountains, and the humans will always come back. Trouble is, it was following the last fire that proved my undoing, and the humans have long memories, I will need to speak to Jobe to keep him safe, not sure if Heti ever told him the story. I guess we will soon find out besides the night is drawing in and soon the darkness will take our sight, and then the darkness will inevitably take my dear Heti, and the heartache will once again return. I have to be strong for the time I have here, with Jobe but that will certainly be limited, for whilst I remain everyone including Jobe will be in danger."

They were nearing the camp, and the anguish facing Scar was telling on his temperament, his face had become gaunt and nervous twitching became more agitated.

The bushes opened out to where the camp lay, by the tree lay Heti she managed to smile through her pain but equally the life began to drain from her. Jobe ran to his father, and as they embraced Scar took him to one side, to explain why he was now here.

"Son, you have grown into a fine bear, I have heard great things about you, they trust you, I trust you, your mother is so very proud of you."

"Dad, mum is not too well at the moment, the fire bit her, and I have to look

after her, till she is better again, I am glad you are here, together we can make her better."

"Son you have been so great with the way you have dealt with the red mist, or fire as we know it, but you have to understand, that at times you fail to see what lies before you. Yes you have been great with your mum, but that fire not only took her fur but is right now eating away at her soul, the fire rarely has any mercy and that is what you need to understand. Your mother is far from well, she had to remain positive for all you sakes, and for that I am so very proud of her, but like the seasons, they come and go, soon you mother will pass over to the other side, all we can do now is make her comfortable"

The reality of the message had taken Jobe by surprise; tears filled his eyes as he cast a loving glance across to where she lay.

"Tears are fine but you have to be strong now for her, for us, and for you, nothing can stop the sorrow that will soon engulf her, there will be time for reflection, but there will be no happy ending to this sorry tale. As you well know, I have a limited time to spend with you, the humans are sure to return, you have to be brave, you need to understand that life is seldom easy. Do not fall into the trap that I did, food will be scarce but keep away from the humans, the forest will always provide and you are the provider. Soon night will take your mother we have to be brave, both of us, I have known you mother many years and through many seasons, but now you need to forge your own future, and live the best life you can."

Jobe now had a choice as to how he should handle the upcoming sorrow. He could not let it affect the way he has kept it together, not just for him but for everyone, time was limited and both Scar and Jobe would spend the time as a family, something he had always dreamed of.

Deacon came over to talk to both the bears, he had now had a weight lifted off of his shoulders, he never wanted to lie, keep secrets from Jobe but he was torn.

"Scar I hope you are ok with me calling you, it was what Heti wanted, Jobe is young but he has the fight of a king and the will to carry on, I am glad you could make it for I too fear what the night will bring."

"Deacon, you did as you were asked and Heti needed to trust someone and you have proven that you belong here. Jobe may be angry with you for keeping him in the dark but I feel he will understand. You are right I feel the night will take my dearest Heti, but life will go on and with your guidance and help, Jobe will come out of this better prepared for the future. Go and join the rest I have to deal with the emotions of my son and soon his heart will be fragile."

With that the tears began to well up in his eyes but he had to be strong for both Heti and Jobe. He strode across to where Heti lay, in pain and Jobe beside her. her smile was forced but as they lay together the forest fell silent, the night was closing in and the shadows of death lurking behind every tree, the colony was silent and the stench of death loomed.

The moon big and bright in the still tainted sky lit up where the family lay, huddled up as they were aware of the fact that time for Heti was limited, her paws looping them together, she knew her time was near its end. Tears rolled down her face in silence, but the fire had destroyed her spirit, her drive, but the love for her family was never diminished. She cast a glance at her family, and Deacon watched from afar, he was devastated but there was nothing left he could do. He bowed his head to Heti, and said a few silent prayers for them all; he then turned and shuffled away. He feared that Jobe would never forgive him for keeping such a fateful secret from him and decided to leave and find a new life, deeper in the forest, away from the sorrows that had ultimately led to the death of a loved and cherished mother.

The night remained quiet, but as the sun began to rise, it was evident that time had almost run out for Heti. She had but shallow breathing, the light in her eyes dwindled, and Scar knew her last breath was not to far away.

Chapter 10

The Reality of Death

Scar woke Jobe, who lay snuggled up to his mother, "Jobe now is the time to say goodbye to your mother her night will soon be endless but she will be free of all the pain she is in. The fire has burnt out her soul, and now, though sad, it is time for her to let go. Do not be afraid of the sorrow that you soon will feel, it is part of a journey all of us will need to take. You now have to be strong, like she has been these past few days, death will soon be upon us, and life will be difficult, but it will go on."

"Father, are you not able to help extend her life, you have survived for many years, can we not take her into the mountains, where you remain safe?"

"Jobe, no matter where we go we cannot prevent the night from taking her, the fire is an element we have little control of, it has taken so many lives across this forest, and will continue to do so. Humans are more predictable, they use weapons that are invented to maim and kill, like the crocodile traps that hide in the clearings. I survived in the mountains because I am clever and the humans are predictable, not even the mountains can help her now."

Heti reached out for Jobe, and scar, the shadow of death was almost upon her, and though the sun was rising the light of life was draining from her body.

"My darlings, please do not cry, my heart will always be with you both, my time is almost at an end and you have to be strong. Your strength will be measured by the next few days, till you have accepted that life must go on. Jobe, my dear Jobe, do not blame Deacon for keeping my secret, I had no choice, he was following my orders and for that I am so grateful, you and your father are here because of Deacon, it was not easy for him, it would eat away at him, the fact he knew and you were unable to know. Hold my hand for I am cold, so very cold, it is time for me go and you have to be strong. I will remain in your hearts forever and you'll survive the hard journey you now embark on. Shed only tears of joy I can ask no more."

With a long and slow exhale her eyes closed and her heart and soul were released. Both Scar and Jobe let out a cry of sorrow as her body became limp and the night had taken her away.

In the not too distant forest Deacon watched and on hearing the cry of sorrow, he turned and began a journey of sadness, alone for his anguish was trauma. Jobe had looked after the colony and in his eyes he had lied to one who he looked up too, but only time will tell.

"Son we need to prepare a fitting burial for your mum, we cannot wait, soon the humans will return, and they will not take her for their own pride, we can ensure she is always safe from those who choose to interfere. Come let us find a secure and fitting resting place we are running out of time here."

Jobe followed in his father's footsteps, he cast a saddened look at where his mother lay and turned to where they headed.

They headed into the forest, away from where the fire left its trail, Jobe was overcome with sadness but he had to put on a brave face, he did not want his father to know. After a short walk they came across a small island with a shallow path leading to it, the lack of rain this winter had drained the water round one side.

"Son, this will be a fitting place to rest your mother, soon, when the rain returns, she will be encased in water, the humans will not be able to access her final resting place. Come we must now prepare."

Many of the colony agreed to help with the digging of the grave, including Jobe, sad though it was. But soon the grave was large enough to encase his loving mother, and the sun set was the time to put her to rest. Jobe took time out alone, to reflect on all that had happened, and he was stricken with emotion, he cried beside his mum, and talked freely of his sadness, it would soon be time to say a sad farewell to Heti.

The last rays of sunshine painted pictures through the forest, he knew it was time to say farewell, and he wiped tears from his eyes.

"Son, it's time to set you mother's soul free; though it has been burnt by the fire that swallowed half the forest up, it is now time for her soul to leave.

With those few words still echoing through the forest, Scar scooped up Heti's body, and carried her to her final resting place. They all gathered round the small island as the body was laid within in the grave, and silence overcame the forest, not a single sound could be heard. The body was delicately covered over as all the colony shed a tear for the passing of a wonderful mother. Scar said a few words in remembrance

"We gather together in the aftermath of the fire that has raged for many days, it has taken away much of the forest, but it has also taken the heart and soul of our believed Heti. She has had a tough but rewarding life, and since my own exile into the mountains, it is clear she led a great life. She leaves us all with saddened hearts, but it has strengthened our resolve to face the future. It may turn out to be a difficult year, but we have to carry on and fight for our survival.

Food will be scarce but take notice of how things worked out for me, I was weak and I crumbled with the hunger when last the fire raged. Be aware, of the humans that seek to show they are superior to us, we have to live away from those that hunt the animals of our forest, we may have only the bare necessities in the coming year but we will survive. I will soon have to return to the mountains for whilst I am here, you are not safe, they still hunt for me. Jobe is my son and a brave bear, he will need your help and support over the coming months but he has the knowledge to overcome these coming months. We lay the body of our sister to rest, in the solitude of this island away from the prying eyes of the humans but she is safe and will always remain safe. Let us pray."

The forest fell silent as they all said a prayer and they left the island, Jobe remained there his heart sad but he needed to pay his own respect to his devoted mother. From a distance, Deacon watched, the sadness fall, he was all alone in his own grief, and what made it worse was he dare not show his face, for fear of what may happen. Jobe, entered the water on the side that remained flowing, a solemn fish gave up its life as Jobe scooped it out of the water and presented it to the grave, like a token of thanks and lay beside the grave till the morning sun lit up the forest.

The sun was up early but there was a strange aura to the sky, it looked like the smoke had drowned the blue from the sky. In the distance there were storms brewing, after such a dry spring it was looking like at last the rains had come. Jobe knew it was time to leave, the colony watched from afar, Deacon watched all alone, he was deeply saddened that this could be his life, like Scar alienated from a group he chose as his family. He could not as yet leave for the mountain, something Heti said before she passed away, to him in confidence.

"Try as you will to build the bridges of sorrow, time waits for nobody, who gives their support to those who need it most." Deacon knew that soon he would need to face the anger of Jobe, which scared him the most, he had lost a mother he adored and a father running from the humans, nothing could prepare him for that.

The first real rain drops began to fall just after midday, the dark menacing clouds turned day into night, the ferocity of the storm, brought torrents of water through the forest, the island where Heti now lay would soon be inaccessible, but she was safe. The colony of animals huddled together beneath the few remaining trees in the area. They had to wait until the storms had passed, for they knew not where dangers lay, as they were unfamiliar with the contours of this part of the forest but once the rain eased they would need to move. Deacon huddled, cold and alone beneath a bush, shivering, contemplating it was time to move into the mountain, and live the life that Scar was accustomed to, he was sad, so very sad but alone in his sorrow. A rustling close by startled Deacon, briefly he had let his mind switch off and now he feared what horrors lay in wait. He looked for an escape route and was about to run when a soft voice eased his anguish.

"Fear not, I am only hear to help you, I have been watching you, for a while, why are you alone? Your friends they huddle together, but you cower in fear. What is it that scares you so much?"

"Who are you, I have not seen you round these parts, and why are you here?"

"I am one of the forest communicators; you called for the return of Scar and this because you knew that Heti was in a bad way. Nothing in this world would have saved her, the red mist had already taken her soul, you found a way to unite the family in grief, but yet you hide, alone like you are hated. What is it that you fear? Is it the fact you kept what you knew to yourself?"

"Yes, I feel that I betrayed the trust of the only true leader that we had, he would be angry, he will hate me for not telling him, that his mother was dying. That is what I fear."

"Fear and knowledge are one in the same, if you had told Jobe about his mother, then his leadership would have been challenged, he would have stayed, with her, food would have been limited, and the colony would have suffered. It was the right thing to do, Heti knew this and she trusted you, nobody else, you. Remember, what you did was for the colony, there was no other reason, and Heti, knew to trust you, so, go and make your peace it will be difficult but you will be respected for it. "

With those few words all was quiet, and once again he was alone, but still he feared the wrath of Jobe, but kept a close eye on the colony, till he was sure to be able to return and explain the reasons for what he had done.

Deacon was cold and alone but after the thoughts of the forest communicator; he decided to return to the colony, while Scar was still about at least then he felt safer than if Jobe was alone. He walked through the camp, and went to speak to Jobe, it was the right thing to do but he feared him.

"Deacon, where have you been, I looked for you, but could not find you, so where have you been?"

Deacon, held his head, as if ashamed at what he had done, even fear ran through his body.

"Jobe, forgive me, I had little choice, your mum, asked me to keep it from you, but I had no choice, surely you can see that, if, if."

"Deacon, I know that you had to keep it from me, mum told me, I was disappointed, but now I see the reasoning behind what you did, and I am glad you did, Dad also spoke to me and he expressed the same knowledge. We are best as a colony here. without that we are in more danger, but we can as a group face the challenges that we are bound to experience. Dad will help us now, he is here and together we can overcome these challenges together. Come let us rest a while for as sure as night becomes day we will soon have to move on."

Deacon was more settled now and joined in the feast that adorned the grass beneath the shelter that protected from the rain, but Scar was keeping his own secret, soon he would need to return to the mountains, in order to protect the colony. The rain continued throughout the night, and as the new day dawned it was time to move on.

They packed everything away, the last thing anyone wanted was to leave a trail easy to follow, the rain had eased but the rivers ran wild, and Jobe recalled the day he fell in. As they all followed Jobe, they covered many miles in the rain, circling the rapid river to a safe and inviting settlement,

Scar was close but slowly as their new home was in view, he found a way to distance himself from the new home, it was not till later Jobe realised that his father was no longer about. In his heart Jobe already knew his father had started the return to the mountains, but nearer than the old mountain. It was clear he had already a heavy burden with the knowledge that before the end of this day he would be alone, but he had a new colony to concentrate on, to build, and to protect. This was Jobe's time to become an adult in his own right and time will tell if his new and challenging situations would be his making or his undoing. Jobe had grown from a cub to an adult, in such a short time, he had lost his mother; and his father, while he was close enough to help, but for their safety he had no choice but to reside in the mountains.

As the sun began to set, the clouds parted for a few minutes, a growl louder than the thunder echoed across the mountains; in the far distance the silhouette of Scar was visible for few minutes. Jobe stood on his hind legs and growled loudly in return, and then, the clouds and rain descended once more. Home, they had their new home and it was now time for Jobe to lead the colony on their new adventures.

In Loving Memory of a wonderful Mother who
died following a short illness.

COLUMBUS PARK
A Brand New Start

The rain eased, Jobe took himself away from the colony to visit the resting place of his Mother Heti. He sat contemplating across the water which now surrounded the grave where Heti Lay.

The clouds Parted and the sun, so long invisible, it sat in the sky, but it was strange. Never had the sun been such a colour, the sky had and eerie aura, sand whipped up by fierce winds in the south drifted up and mixed with the remnants of the fire still burning in the far south, but slowly dying out.

www.ingramcontent.com/pod-product-compliance
Lightning Source LLC
Chambersburg PA
CBHW081358090726
47908CB00011B/2723